Animal Stories for
Ten Year Olds

Helen Paiba is known as one of the most committed, knowledgeable and acclaimed children's booksellers in Britain. For more than twenty years she owned and ran the Children's Bookshop in Muswell Hill, London, which under her guidance gained a superb reputation for its range of children's books and for the advice available to its customers.

Helen was involved with the Booksellers Association for many years and served on both its Children's Bookselling Group and the Trade Practices Committee. In 1995 she was given honorary life membership of the Booksellers Association of Great Britain and Ireland in recognition of her outstanding services to the association and to the book trade. In the same year the Children's Book Circle (sponsored by Books for Children) honoured her with the Eleanor Farjeon Award, given for distinguished service to the world of children's books.

She retired in 1995 and now lives in London.

Animal
STORIES
for Ten Year Olds

COMPILED BY HELEN PAIBA

ILLUSTRATED BY DAVID FRANKLAND

MACMILLAN
CHILDREN'S BOOKS

First published 2000 by Macmillan Children's Books
a division of Pan Macmillan Limited
20 New Wharf Road, London N1 9RR
Basingstoke and Oxford
www.panmacmillan.com
Associated companies throughout the world

ISBN 0 330 39128 3

3 5 7 9 8 6 4 2

A CIP catalogue record for this book is available
from the British Library.

Typeset by SX Composing DTP, Rayleigh, Essex
Printed and bound in Great Britain by
Mackays of Chatham plc, Kent

Contents

The White Horse of Zennor

Michael Morpurgo

The family had farmed the land in the Foage Valley at Zennor for over five hundred years. They had been there it was said ever since Miguel Veluna first crawled ashore half-drowned at Porthzennor Cove from the wreck of his galleon off Gunnards Head. As soon as he could make himself understood, so the story goes, he married the farmer's daughter who had just nursed him back to life; and with her came the farm in the fertile valley that runs down from the north coast to the south with the high moors rising on either side.

Through the generations the Velunas prospered, sowing their corn along the sheltered fields and grazing their hardy cattle on the moors above. They became tough and circumspect, as are all the farmers whose roots lie deep in the rocks and soil of Penwith, the last bastion of land against the mighty Atlantic that seeks with every storm to subdue the peninsula and to rejoin the Channel a few short miles to the south. Over the centuries the family had survived famine and disease, invasion and depression; but now the Velunas were staring ruin in the face and there seemed no way forward for them.

Farmer Veluna had been a joyful soul all his life, a man of laughter, who rode high through the fields on his tractor, forever singing his heart out, in a perpetual celebration that he belonged where he was. His joy in life was infectious so that he spread around him a convivial sense of security and happiness. In business he was always fair although he was thought to be over-generous at times, not hard enough a man according to some of the more craggy moorland farmers. But no one in the parish was better respected and liked than Farmer Veluna so that when he married lovely Molly Parson from Morvah and produced a daughter and a son within two years, everyone thought it was no more than he deserved.

When he built a new milking parlour some of his friends shook their heads and wondered, for no one could recall a milking herd on the land before; but they knew Farmer Veluna to be level-headed and hard-working. No one doubted that if anyone could make it work he could, and certainly everyone wished him well in his new venture.

For several years the milk flowed and the profits came. He built up the finest herd of Guernsey cows for miles around and there was talk that he was doing so well that he might take on more land. Then, within six short weeks he was a ruined man. First the corn harvest failed completely, a summer storm lashing through the valley breaking the ripened corn and flattening it to the ground. The storm was followed by weeks of heavy drizzle so that not even the straw could be salvaged. But the cows were still milking and the regular milk cheque was always there every month to see them through. Farmer Veluna was disappointed by the set-back but burned off the straw when he could and began to plough again. He was still singing on his tractor.

Then came the annual Ministry check for brucellosis (a highly contagious disease that kills calves before they are born), the outcome of which had never worried Farmer Veluna. It was routine, no more than that, so that when the two vets arrived at his front door some days later it never even occurred to him that they had come about the brucellosis test. The vets knew him well and liked him for he was good to his stock and paid his bills, so they broke the news to him as gently as they could. Farmer Veluna stood in the doorway, his heart heavy with fore-boding as they began to tell him the worst.

"There can be no mistake?" he said. "You're sure there's no mistake?" But he knew he need not have asked.

"It's brucellosis, Farmer, no doubt about it; right through the herd. I'm sorry, but you know what has to be done," said one of the vets, putting a hand on his shoulder to comfort him. "It has to be done today. The Ministry men are on their way. We've come to help." Farmer Veluna nodded slowly and they went inside together.

That afternoon his entire herd of golden Guernseys was driven into the yard below the dairy and killed. Every cow and calf on the farm, even one born that same morning, was slaughtered; and the milking parlour stood silent from that day on.

In the weeks that followed the disaster every tractor and saleable machine had to be sold for there was the family to feed as well as the other stock, and an overdraft at the bank that Farmer Veluna had to honour. It was not much money to find each month but with little coming in, it soon became apparent that the pigs had to be sold, then the geese and finally the beloved horse. All that was left were a few hens and a shed full of redundant rusting machinery.

Each evening the family would sit around the

kitchen table and talk over the possibilities, but as the situation worsened the children noticed that it was their mother who emerged the stronger. The light had gone out of their father's eye, his entire demeanour was clouded over with despair. Even his jaunty, lurruping walk had slowed, and he moved aimlessly around the farm now as if in a daze. He seemed scarcely even willing or able to consider any suggestions for the future. His wife, Molly, managed to persuade him to go to the bank to ask for an extension of the loan, and for a new loan to finance new stock and seed; but times were hard even for the banks and when both were refused he lapsed into a profound depression that pervaded every room in the house.

Friends and neighbours came with offers of help but he thanked them kindly for their generosity and refused them politely as they knew he would, for he was above all a proud man from a proud family and not accustomed to accepting charity from anyone, however dire the necessity.

Desperately Molly urged him on, trying to release him from the prison of his despair, believing in her heart that he had it in him to recover and knowing that without him they were lost. The two children meanwhile sought their own consolation and relief up on the high moors they knew and loved so well.

They would leave the house and farm behind them, and climb up to the great granite cheesewring rocks above the village where the wind blew in so fiercely from the sea that they could lean into it with arms outstretched and be held and buffeted like kites. They would leap from rock to rock like mountain goats, play endless hide-and-seek and tramp together over the boggy moors, all the while trying to forget the threat that hung over them. Their walks would end often on the same logan stone above the Eagle's Nest, a giant slab of rounded granite as finely balanced as a pair of scales on the rock below, so that if they stood on opposite ends they could rock it up and down like a seesaw.

Here they were sitting one early autumn evening with the sun setting fire to the sea beyond Zennor when they saw their father and mother climbing up through the bracken towards them. Unusually, they were holding hands and that signified to both children that a decision might have been reached. They instinctively sensed what the decision was and dreaded it. Annie decided she would forestall them.

"You needn't tell us," Annie said to them as they climbed up to sit down beside the children on the logan stone. "We know already. There's no other way is there?"

"What do you know, Annie?" Farmer Veluna, the

6

first words either of the children had heard him utter for more than a week.

"That we're going to sell the farm," she said softly, almost as if she did not wish to hear it. "We're going to sell the farm and move away, aren't we?"

"I won't go," said Arthur, shrugging off his mother's arm. "I won't. I was born here and I'm going to stay here. No one is going to make me move."

He spoke with grim resolve.

At nine, he was a year younger than his sister but at that moment he seemed suddenly a great deal older. He was already as tall as Annie, and even as an infant others had recognized in him that strong Veluna spirit.

"We shall have to sell, Arthur," said his father. "We've no alternative. You need money to run a farm and we haven't got any. It's that simple. Everything we had was in the cows and now they're gone. I'm not going to argue about it; there's no point. We shall have to sell up and buy a smaller farm elsewhere. That's all there is to it. There's other farms and there's other places."

"Not like this one," Arthur said, and turned to his father, tears filling his eyes. "There's no place like this place and you know it. So don't pretend. You told me often enough, Father; you told me never to give up and now you're giving up yourself." Farmer

7

Veluna looked away, unable to give his son any answers that would convince even himself.

"That's unkind, Arthur," said his mother. "You mustn't be unkind to your father, not now. He's done all he can – you know he has. It'll be all right. It'll be the same. We shall go on farming, but in a smaller way, that's all. It's all your father can do; you must see that, Arthur."

Annie turned to her father and put her arms around him as much to comfort herself as to comfort him. It seemed to do neither.

Farmer Veluna stroked his daughter's hair gently.

"We shall be all right, Annie," he said. "I promise you that. Don't worry, I'm not a man to break my promises. You know that, don't you?"

Annie nodded into his chest, fighting back her tears.

"We'll see you back home, children," Molly said. "Don't be long now. It gets cold up here when the sun's gone."

The two children sat side by side and watched their parents move slowly back down the hill towards the farm. They were so alike to look at that many people considered them to be twins. Both had their parents' dark shining hair and their skins stayed dark even in the winter. They had few friends besides each other for there were not many children of their own age on other farms round about, and so they had spent much of their life together, and by now sensed each other's mood intuitively.

"Annie," Arthur said finally when he had wiped the tears away from his cheeks. "I couldn't live anywhere else, could you? We have to find a way to stay here, because I'm not going. I don't care what Father says, I'm not going."

But Annie was not listening to her brother, for she had been distracted some moments before by the sound of a distant voice from behind her, perhaps from the direction of the Quoit. She had thought it might be the wind at first, moaning through the stones. She put her hand on her brother's arm.

"Listen," she said. And the voice was still there, clearly discernible now that Arthur had stopped talking. It was more distinctive now, and although they could as yet make out no words, they could tell that someone was calling out for help. They leapt from the logan stone and ran down the track into the heather and bracken of the high moor, homing in all the while on the plaintive cry that came to them ever more urgently from across the moor. They could hear now that it came from the ruins of the old count-house, and they slowed to a walk as they approached, suddenly uncertain of themselves.

"Help me, please help me." Clearly a man's voice,

a man in pain; and no longer a shout into the wilderness, but a plea directed to them.

"Can you see anyone?" Annie said, clutching Arthur's arm in fright.

"I'm down here, over here in the ruins. Oh for pity's sake, come quickly." The children climbed slowly down into the ruin itself, Annie still holding on to her brother, and at last they found what they had been looking for.

Lying in the corner of the ruined old count-house, propped up against a granite pillar was an old man, but no ordinary man; for he was smaller than any dwarf but unlike a dwarf his features were in perfect proportion to his size. He was roughly clothed in heavy tweed trousers and a black moleskin jacket. He had wild white hair and eyes as blue as the sea. He lay with one knee clasped to his chest and the children saw that clinging grotesquely to his foot was a rusty gin trap.

"A Knocker," Annie whispered, and she stepped back in alarm, dragging Arthur back with her; but Arthur wrenched himself free and stood his ground.

"I know that," Arthur said, speaking loudly for he felt it was rude to whisper. "There's nothing wrong with Knockers. They won't hurt you, 'less you hurt them. Isn't that right, sir?"

"Quite right, young fellow," said the old man

crisply, "and anyway since I'm pinioned here with this confounded trap, there's not too much danger of my hurting you my girl, now is there?"

Annie shook her head vigorously but was not convinced.

"And since you're here I wonder, would it be too much trouble to ask you to help me out of this thing? I would have done it myself if I could, but I'm a wee bit little to pull the spring back and if I move, my leg burns like hell fire. Confounded farmers," he went on, wincing in pain, "they're still trapping you know, but it's not as bad as it was. In the old days my father told me the whole moor was littered with them – rabbit traps, bird traps, fox traps, all sort. You

11

couldn't go out at dark, you know, for fear of putting your foot in it, so to speak. This is an old one, been here for years I should think, but there's still some of them at it. I've seen them. I known everything that goes on. Confounded farmers."

"I'm a farmer's son," said Arthur defensively, crouching down to examine the trap, "and my father wouldn't use gin traps. He says they're cruel and anyway they're not allowed any more."

"Quite right," the Knocker said, straightening out his leg for Arthur. "I know your father. He's a good man. Know you two as well – seen you often enough springing around out on those rocks. Didn't know I was watching, did you? 'Course it's a shame about your farm, but that's life. Swings and roundabouts, ups and downs. It happens."

"You've watched us?" said Annie, who had plucked up enough courage at last to come closer. "You've seen us up there?"

"'Course I have," said the Knocker. "We know everyone for miles around. It's our job to know what's going on; that's what we're here for. Now look, children, can we continue this discussion after you've set me free, if you don't mind. My leg's throbbing and I'll bleed to death if you don't help me out of this soon."

Rust had stiffened the spring so it took Arthur and

Annie some time to prise open the jaws of the trap far enough for the Knocker to withdraw his boot. He fell back to the ground in a faint as the boot came clear. By the time he came to, some minutes later, he found the children had taken his boot off and were kneeling over him bathing his ankle with a wet handkerchief. He lifted himself on to his elbows and smiled up at them.

"That was kind of you," he said. "I'm surprised you didn't run away; most people would have, you know. I think you must know about us. Someone must've told you. But you didn't know we bled, did you?"

Arthur shook his head. "No, but everyone's heard about you," he said, "although no one really believes in you any more. But ever since my mother told us all about Knockers and little people and all that, I've always thought that if you were true then you'd live up here on the moor or maybe down the mines. There's nowhere else for you, is there?"

"I still don't think I should really believe it," said Annie, tying the handkerchief in a tight knot, "if I wasn't touching you, I'm sure I wouldn't."

"The leg will be fine now, right as rain, good as new," said the Knocker.

His pale face was deeply lined with age and there was a kindness and a wisdom in his face that both the children trusted instinctively.

"Thank you," he said as the children helped him to his feet.

He shook them each solemnly by the hand.

"Thank you both very kindly. I don't think I should have survived a frosty autumn night out here on the moor. I'm old, you see, and even Knockers die when they get old, you know. It's so nice to find people who'll talk to us. So many people just run away and it's such a pity, because there's nothing to be frightened of."

He hobbled unaided around the ruined count-house testing his leg before returning to the children.

"No broken bones I think. All's well that ends well, as they say."

"Will you be all right now?" Arthur asked. "We ought to be getting back home now. Father said we should be off the moor by dark."

"Quite right. Wise man, your father," the little Knocker said, brushing off his moleskin jacket and pulling it down straight. "After all, you never know who you might bump into up here. The place is full of spriggans and pixies and nasty wee little folk and even," he whispered low, "even the odd Knocker or two." And the three laughed together as old friends might do over a confidential joke. "But before you go, children, I have to thank you properly. One good turn deserves another, tit for tat, you scratch my back, I'll scratch yours, and so on. I want each of you to close your eyes and tell me your one dearest wish. You have to say what you'd most like in all the world. Ask and you shall have it. Annie, you're first. Come on now."

Annie did not have to think for long.

"A horse," she said, her eyes squeezed tight shut. "We had to sell our horse, you see, because Father needed the money for the farm. I've always wanted a great white horse."

"Keep your eyes closed," said the Knocker. "Keep them closed both of you and don't open them until I tell you. Now you, Arthur. What is it that you'd most want in all the world?"

"I want to stay here on the farm," said Arthur slowly. "I want my father to be happy again and to go singing on his tractor. I want the animals back and the farm working again like it used to."

"That's a lot of wants," said the Knocker. "Let's see what we can do now."

He chucked aloud, and his voice seemed more animated now.

"You know, children, I haven't had the chance to do this for donkey's years. I'm so excited, I feel like a little Knocker all over again. You wished for a horse, Annie; and you wished for the farm back as it was,

15

Arthur. How you do it is up to you, but you'll find enough seed corn in the barn when you get back home and you can use the horse as you wish. But after a year and a day you must bring the horse back here to me and leave twelve sacks of good seed corn back in your barn to repay me. Do you understand? Remember, be back here by dusk a year and a day from now."

"We'll be here," said Arthur.

"Promise?" said the Knocker.

"We promise," they said solemnly.

"You should be able to manage everything by that time with luck, and I'll see you have enough of that. All right children, open your eyes now."

In place of the little Knocker stood a giant of a horse, towering above them, a brilliant white from mane to tail. He looked down at the children almost casually, swished his tail, shook his head with impatience and then sprang out over the ruined wall and on to the open moor beyond, where he stood waiting in the bracken for the scrambling children to catch him up.

Arthur had never been fond of horses. They seemed to him to be unpredictable creatures and he had always steered clear of them. Anyway, as a budding farmer he had no use for any animal that was not productive. But Annie had enough

16

confidence and experience for both of them and she caught him gently by the mane and stroked his nose, speaking softly to him all the while.

Within a few minutes they were both mounted on the great white horse and were trotting down the hillside and into the farmyard where the chickens scattered in panic at their approach. The noise brought Farmer Veluna and Molly running out of the back door where they were faced with the terrifying spectacle of their two children perched precariously up on a massive white stallion of at least seventeen hands, that snorted in excitement, tossing its head and pawing the yard, sending sparks flying along the cobbles into the dark.

Arthur told their story breathlessly. With the evidence of the horse before their eyes and the obvious sincerity in Arthur's voice, it was difficult for his father or mother to harbour any doubts but that the story was indeed true. Certainly they knew Arthur had a wild and fertile imagination and was impetuous enough at times but with Annie sitting astride the horse in front of them, laughing aloud with delight and adding her own details from time to time, both Farmer Veluna and Molly were very soon completely convinced.

"Look in the barn, Father," Arthur proclaimed with absolute confidence. "The little man said there'd be enough seed corn in there to make a start. We can save the farm, Father, I know we can. The seed will be there, I'm sure of it. Have a look, Father."

Farmer Veluna crossed the yard on his own and opened wide the great barn doors. They saw the light go on, bathing the yard in a yellow glow, and they heard a whoop of joy before Farmer Veluna came running out again. He was laughing as he used to laugh.

"Well I'll eat my hat," he said, and stuffed the peak of his flat cap into his mouth. Annie and Arthur knew then they had found their father again. "We have a horse and we have the seed," Farmer Veluna said. "There's all my father's old horsedrawn equipment in the old cart shed, and I think I know where I can find his old set of harness. It's up in the attic, isn't it, Molly?" But he did not wait for a reply. "It may be a bit small for this giant of a horse, but it'll stretch. It'll fit – it's got to fit. 'Course, I've never worked a horse, but Father did and I watched him years ago and followed him often enough in the fields. I'll pick it up; it shouldn't be too difficult. We've a chance," he said. "We've a chance, children, a sporting chance."

And from that moment on there was no more talk of selling up.

*

Ploughing started the following morning just after dawn. The ground was just dry enough, the earth turning cleanly from the shares. The horse proved tireless in the fields. They had sold every bale of hay so he had to pick enough sustenance from the cold wet autumn grass; but that seemed to be enough for him, for the horse ploughed on that day well into the evening, and came back for more the next day and the next and the next.

It was clear at the outset that the horse had an uncanny instinct for the land. He knew how tight to turn, what speed to go without ever having to be told. When his father tired, Arthur could walk behind the plough and simply follow the horse down the furrows and around the headlands until the job was done. If he stumbled and fell in the furrows, as he often did, the horse would wait for him to regain his feet before leaning again into his harness, taking the strain and plodding off down the field.

Within three weeks all the corn fields along the valley were ploughed, harrowed and drilled with barley. Word spread quickly around the parish that Farmer Veluna was laughing again and they came visiting once more to stand at the gate with him and admire his miraculous workhorse.

"No diesel, nothing to go wrong; he'll plough the steepest land on the farm," Farmer Veluna would say with expansive pride. "Built like a tank but gentle as a lamb. See for yourself. Arthur can manage him on his own and he's only nine, you know. Have you ever seen anything like it?"

"Where the devil did you get him from?" they would ask because they had heard all kinds of rumours.

And he would tell them the story of the little Knocker man on the moor who had come to their rescue, but no one believed him. The farmers amongst them laughed knowingly at the story and told Farmer Veluna to pull the other one; but they did not press him for they knew well enough that a farmer will never disclose the source of his good fortune. But at home their wives knew better and the story of the amazing white horse of Zennor spread along the coast like thistledown in the wind.

But in spite of their scepticism, all their friends were delighted to see Farmer Veluna his old self again, and they determined to help him succeed. So one winter's night in the Tinner's Arms they got together and worked out how they might help the farmer back on his feet whether he wanted their help or not. They knew he was proud, as they were, so that any help had to be both anonymous and unreturnable.

So it was that on Christmas morning when Farmer

Veluna and his family returned home after church, they found their yard filled with milling animals: three sows and a boar, half a dozen geese, five cows with suckling calves and at least twenty-five ewes. Puzzled and not a little suspicious, Farmer Veluna phoned all around the parish to find out who owned the wandering animals that had converged on his yard, but no one seemed to know anything about them and no one claimed them. He was about to contact the police in Penzance when Arthur and Annie came running into the kitchen, their voices shrill with excitement.

"The barn," Annie shouted. "It's full, full of hay and straw."

"And there's feed," Arthur said. "Sacks and sacks of it, enough to last us through the winter."

"It's that Knocker again," Farmer Veluna said, and the children believed him; but Molly, with a woman's intuition, knew better but said nothing.

The winter was long and hard that year, but with the sounds of the farm all around them again and the winter corn shooting up green in the fields, Farmer Veluna and his family were more than content. The white horse wintered out in a sheltered field behind the old granary. He grew a long white shaggy coat so that he seemed even more vast than ever. Whenever he was not needed hauling the dung cart or carrying

22

hay bales out to the cattle on the farm, Annie would ride him out over the moor and down through the fields to the cliffs. He was of course far too big for her to control, but she had no fear of horses and found that no control was needed anyway. A gentle word in his ear, a pat of encouragement on his great arching neck and he would instantly do what she wanted. It was not obedience and Annie recognized that; it was simply that the horse wished to please her. He would go like the wind, jump any ditch or fence he was asked to and seemed as sure-footed on the hills as a goat.

But it was on one of these rides that Annie first discovered that he had an inclination to make his way towards the cliffs, and once there he would stand looking out to the open sea, ears pricked to the cry of the wheeling gulls and the thunder of the surf against the cliffs. He was always reluctant to turn away for home, calling out at the last over his shoulder and turning back his ears as if expecting some kind of reply.

After just such a ride Annie finally decided upon a name for the horse. No name seemed to have suited until now. "He'll be called Pegasus," she declared, and no one argued for she had become vehemently possessive, scolding both Arthur and her father if they worked him too hard on the farm or did not look after him as well as she thought they should have done. She groomed him regularly every morning and picked out his feet. She it was who towelled him down after work and rubbed in the soothing salted water so that the harness would not make him sore. She was passionately proud of him and would ride tall through the village when she rode out with the hunt, soaking in the admiration and envy of both riders and spectators alike.

There was not a horse in the parish to touch him and even other horses seemed to sense it, moving nervously away whenever he approached. There were some who doubted that any horse could jump just as well as he could plough, but when they witnessed his performance in the chase any doubts vanished at once. Where others pulled aside to find a lower hedge or a narrower ditch, Pegasus sailed over with apparent ease. He out-paced every horse in the field and Annie used no whip and no spur, for none were needed. He was, she said glowingly when she got back home, as strong as any tractor, as bold as a hunter, and as fast as a racehorse. Pegasus had become a local celebrity and Annie basked in his reflected glory.

With the spring drying out the land Pegasus turned carthorse once more and was hitched up for the spring ploughing. Farmer Veluna had enough seed for two small fields of oats and Pegasus went to it with a will; but both Arthur and his father now noticed that the horse would pause, ears pricked, at the end of the furrow nearest to the sea; and it was quite apparent that the furrows going down the hill towards the cliffs in the distance were sometimes ploughed more quickly and therefore less deeply than the furrows leading back to the farmhouse.

"Most horses speed up on the way back home; that's what I thought," said Farmer Veluna. "Can't understand it, it doesn't make sense."

"But you can't expect him to behave like an ordinary horse, Father," said Arthur, "'cos he isn't an ordinary horse. Just look at him, Father, he'd plough this field all on his own if you let him. Go on, Father, try it, let him do it."

Farmer Veluna let go of the plough more to please his son than anything else and allowed the horse to move on alone. As they watched in amazement the plough remained straight as an arrow, an inch perfect in depth. Pegasus turned slowly and came back towards them, his line immaculate and parallel. Arthur and his father picked the stones out of the furrows as evening fell while Pegasus ploughed up and down the field until the last furrow was complete. Then they ran over the field towards him to guide him round the headlands, but Pegasus had already turned and was making the first circuit of the field. At that moment both Arthur and his father finally understood what Annie already knew, that this was a miraculous creature that needed no help from them or from anyone.

Annie fitted in her rides whenever she thought Pegasus was rested enough after his work, but as the blackthorn withered and the fuchsia began to bud in the early summer, Pegasus was more and more occupied on the farm. At the end of June he cut a fine crop of sweet meadow hay, turned it and baled it. He took cartloads of farmyard manure out into the fields for spreading. He cut thistles and docks and bracken in the steeper fields up near the moor. Hitched up with a great chain he pulled huge granite rocks out of the grounds and dragged them into the hedgerows. In the blazing heat of high summer he hauled the water tanks out on to the furthest fields and in August harvested the corn he had drilled the autumn before.

The barley crop was so rich that summer that Farmer Veluna was able to sell so much to the merchants that he could buy in more suckling cows and calves, as well as his first ten milking cows, the beginnings of his new dairy herd. As autumn began the milking parlour throbbed into life once more, but he had not forgotten to keep back twelve sacks of seed corn that he owed to the little Knocker.

The sows had farrowed well and there were already fat pigs to sell; and some of the lambs were already big enough to go to market. The hens were laying well, even in the heat, and the goslings would be ready for Christmas.

But in spite of the recovery and all it meant to the family, the mood of the farmhouse was far from happy, for as the summer nights shortened and the blackberries ripened in the hedgerows, they knew that their year with Pegasus was almost over. Annie spent all her time now with him, taking him out every day for long rides down to the cliffs where she knew he loved to be. Until dusk each evening she would sit astride him, gazing with him out to sea, before turning him away and walking slowly up Trevail Valley, through Wicca Farm and back home over the moor.

When the time came that September evening, a year and a day from the first meeting with the Knocker, Annie and Arthur led the horse by his long white mane up on to the high moors. Arthur wanted to comfort his sister for he could feel the grief she was suffering. He said nothing but he put his hand into hers and clasped it tight. As they neared the cheesewring rocks and moved out along the track across the moor towards the ruined count house, Pegasus lifted his head and whinnied excitedly. There was a new spring in his step and his ears twitched back and forth as they approached the count house. Annie let go of his mane and whispered softly. "Off you go, Pegasus," she said. Pegasus looked down at her as if reassuring himself that she meant what she said, and then trotted out ahead of them and down into the ruins until he was hidden from view. The children followed him, clambering laboriously over the walls.

As they dropped down into the count house they saw that the horse was gone and in his place was the little old Knocker, who waved to them cheerily. "Good as your word," he said.

"So were you," Arthur said. "Father is a happy man again and it won't be long before we'll be milking fifty cows like we were before. Father says we'll be able to afford a tractor soon."

"Where's he gone?" Annie asked in a voice as composed as her tears would allow. "Where's Pegasus gone?"

"Out there," said the Knocker pointing out to sea. "Look out there. Can you see the white horses playing, d'you see their waving manes? Can you hear them calling? Don't be sad, Annie," he said kindly. "He loves it out there with his friends. A year on the land was a year of exile for him. But you were so good to him, Annie, and for that reason he'll come back to you this one night in every year. That's a promise. Be here up on the moor and he'll come every year for as long as you want him to."

And he does come, one autumn night in every year as the old Knocker promised. So if you happen to be walking up towards Zennor Quoit one moon-bright autumn night with the mists hovering over the valley and the sea shining below the Eagle's Nest, and if you hear the pounding of hoof beats and see a white horse come out of the moon and thunder over the moor, you will know that it is Annie – Annie and the white horse of Zennor.

David and the Kittens

Robert Westall

The kittens were no more. It was like a death in Gran's house. David sat and swung his legs in the awful silence, and thought how it all began. Was it only three months ago?

"Furble's getting fat," said David.

"Furble's having kittens," said Gran.

"Shall we have to have the vet?" asked David, alarmed.

"Lord love you, no. She'll know what to do. She's a farm-cat born and bred. And a grand ratter. They say good ratters make good mothers."

Furble grew fatter.

"She's shaped like a *pear*," said David.

"She's like a pod," said Gran. "A pod full of peas. Feel. Gently. You can feel all the little heads."

David counted four.

Then suddenly Furble sat up with her front legs splayed and her ears and eyes going every which way.

"They're kicking her," said Gran. David stared at the tiny explosions under Furble's white belly-fur. And the bewilderment on Furble's face.

"Are you sure she'll know what to do?"

"Just you wait," said Gran.

As the days passed, Furble gave up ratting. She just sat and washed and washed her white belly-fur. Bare pink patches began appearing.

"She's wearing her fur away licking," said David.

"That's so the kittens will know where to feed," said Gran. "Look, you can see her nipples clear."

When Furble had grown so fat she couldn't *grow* any fatter, Gran got the usual place ready – the bottom drawer of the kitchen cupboard. She lined it with plain paper. "Not newsprint," said Gran. "We don't want newsprint coming off on their fur. I hope she takes to the drawer. Young cats can be so silly their first time. Welly had hers on a shelf ten feet from the ground. We had a rare time searching for them, when she strolled in all skinny one morning."

Furble sat in the shadowed part of the drawer, looking broody. The other she-cats looked in over the top. But one look from Furble was enough to send them away again. She began to pant, and then tried to climb out of the drawer on to Gran's knee.

"They'll have them on your knee, if you let them,"

said Gran. "If they're fond of you." She put Furble back firmly, but went and sat on the floor by the drawer, and stroked the cat. "They like their humans near."

Then suddenly Furble shuddered and kicked out her back legs backwards, and there was a transparent sausage on the end of a string. With a kitten trapped inside, a struggling, heaving sausage of head and legs, all glistening.

"What do we do?" yelled David.

"Watch," said Gran.

Furble doubled round like a hoop. Her white teeth flashed on the struggling sausage.

"She's killing it. She's eating it," shouted David. "Help."

But the next second the sausage was empty, and a tiny wet mouse-like thing was feebly struggling on the wet paper, towards the bulk of its mother. And Furble's huge tongue was licking it on and helping it. David had never seen anything so weak and helpless.

"Four," said Gran. "I thought there were four. Two little ginger toms, a black tom, and a little white female, I reckon. Anyway, I can guess who the fathers were . . ."

"Fathers?"

"Four kittens can have four different fathers," said Gran.

Just then Furble got up and leapt out of the drawer, sending squeaking kittens flying in all directions. She flew out of the cat flap.

"To relieve the calls of nature," said Gran. "But watch the kittens."

Squeaking loudly, the kittens were rolling about the wet paper. Blind, helpless, tiny legs flailing hopelessly. And yet, by some miracle, within a minute they were all back in one tiny squirming heap.

"Why," gasped David. "How?"

"To keep warm, and not to be alone. They're all they know, when their mum's away. And they do it all by hearing each other, because they're blind. Once they're together they're quiet."

The kittens grew, and grew further. Slowly their ears, folded to their skulls, opened like little petals. Behind their slits, the blind eyes bulged and moved. Their tails, from being thin and rat-like, grew into fat little triangles. They lay on an old blanket in the drawer now. A blanket full of valleys, folds and creases. David had invented a game. As soon as Furble and Gran left the kitchen, he picked up the kittens from their tight wriggling heap, and put one in each corner of the drawer. Immediately, their squeaking started. And then, still blind, by rolling, falling, crawling, paddling along their fat bodies with tiny legs, they found each other again, and the squeaking stopped, and the wriggling of the heap started again.

"Why do they never stop wriggling?"

"To get into the middle where it's warmest. And *don't* pick them up too much, or they'll smell of you, not Furble. Then she might reject them. She might even *kill* them."

David felt guilty.

On the tenth day, Gran said, "Watch their eyes. They should open today. Once their ears are up, their eyelids split."

And by the evening, some kittens had one-and-a-half eyes open, and others no more than a glinting slit.

"Must watch those eyes," said Gran. "This is when wild kittens get eye infections and go blind. See how much Furble is licking their eyes. There's antiseptic in her spit."

But the oddest thing was, once the kittens' eyes were open, they refused to stay in their tight squirming ball, and began endless meandering crawls round the drawer. Just like ants on the patio outside . . . Furble kept picking them up by the scruff of the neck, and putting them back in the heap.

"Now her troubles are starting," said Gran.

It was the black kitten who got out of the drawer first. He'd been trying for ages to claw up the side. Suddenly, he was on top and had fallen off with a flop on to the kitchen tiles, and then he began squealing for his mother.

Furble rescued him by the scruff, carried him back in, and, holding him down with a heavy paw, washed him 'til he squealed again.

"They'll all be out tomorrow," said Gran. "We won't be able to move for kittens. God help her. They'll drive her frantic."

*

David watched the kittens feeding. "They don't like each other much," he said. "They're clawing each other away from the nipples. They're trampling on each other's faces."

"Like each other?" said Gran. "You wait."

"Why do the kittens never do poo?" said David.

"Well," said Gran, "if they did poo all over the drawer, Furble would have to keep finding a new home for them. Cats are very clean and she just licks them on their rear ends and that keeps them clean until they are big enough to crawl by themselves to a place they choose to poo. That's why kittens are so easy to house-train. You just make sure they use the litter-tray when they are big enough – put them on to it, they'll soon learn."

Now the kittens were moving everywhere. They flew around the kitchen as erratically as autumn leaves, far better at moving than in knowing where they were going. Furble kept on picking them up, and returning them to the drawer, and they kept escaping again. She was frantic.

"She's like the old woman who lived in a shoe. She has so many children she doesn't know what to do. I'll put them in the old tea-chest to give her a bit of peace."

David eyed the towering sides of the tea-chest. "They'll never get out of that."

"I'll give them two days. Two days of peace for her. Two days of peace for us." Two days it was.

"Now's the time to find them homes," said Gran.

"But they're far too young to leave her."

"People who want kittens like to be in at the beginning. They like to come every week and see how their kitten's getting on. Here you are – magazines." She pushed a foot-high pile of magazines at David. "We're looking for pictures of kittens. Coloured pictures."

It was amazing how many pictures David found. Even in the *TV Times*.

"Five postcards," said Gran. "One each for the Post Office, the off-licence, the vet's, the corner-shop and the pet shop in town."

She stuck on each two pictures of ginger toms, one of a black kitten and one of a little white female. Then she took up a red felt-tip and wrote on each card: "VERY GOOD HOMES WANTED FOR ADORABLE KITTENS."

"All kittens are adorable," she said. "People just need reminding." Then she listed them.

"'ROMULUS AND REMUS'. TWIN GINGER TOMS.

'LUCKY'. A LUCKY BLACK TOM.
'SNOWDROP'. A PRETTY WHITE FEMALE."

"Why'd you give them names? People will want to given them their own names."

"I know they will," said Gran. "I once called a pair of tabby toms 'Starsky' and 'Hutch', but the people who took them called them 'Benson' and 'Hedges'. But it all helps to make the postcard more interesting. It'll be the female we'll have trouble finding a home for. Toms are easier to have 'done' and it costs less. But females make the best mousers and ratters, if people did but know it."

She gave David a pound coin. "Run down to the shops with the postcards. Don't give them the money until they've put the card in the window. Two weeks in each shop. That should do it."

And it did.

The phone rang two nights later. The family came round. Gran gave them coffee, and everybody sat round the kitchen, while the kittens wavered and wobbled round their feet.

"I'd like the little white one," said the little girl, cradling it to her cheek. Her mum looked worried. Very worried.

"I've always wanted a lucky black cat," she said at last.

"I've always fancied ginger toms," said the father.

"I think you're very wise," said Gran. "They'll be good company for each other. They'll have you in fits with their antics." She gave the father her most winning smile.

After that there wasn't much argument. The family departed asking if they could come back in a week, to see how their kittens were getting on.

"I like kittens to go in pairs," said Gran. "It's terrible what happens to single kittens. One day they've got their mum and all their brothers and sisters, and the next they're all alone among strangers. That's when you've got to love them and cuddle them non-stop or —"

"Or what?"

"Or else they turn into very dull cats, who just don't like anybody. I've seen too many cats like that."

A couple came at the weekend. And chose the lucky black tom. Oddly, they liked the name "Lucky". But they didn't want the little white female, and nor, it seemed, did anybody else. David began to worry. What if they couldn't find a home? "Oh well," said Gran, "maybe we'll keep her for ourselves. Trouble is, that way, I could end up one of those ladies with twenty cats. It's very easily done, you know, if you're soft-hearted and people know it. 'Snowdrop' could be having kittens of her own before long. Four months old when they start. Nature can be very cruel."

But it got forgotten in the fun of the riotous time. What Gran called "thunder-of-hooves-time". Kittens chasing each other everywhere, leaping on each other, crashing each other down, biting each other's necks until squeals became piteous. Lying in ambush, waggling their tiny bottoms, pouncing.

"They're practising killing each other," said Gran, swiftly rescuing Snowdrop, who was getting the worst of things.

Kittens could do so many things cats couldn't. Running sideways like crabs, running backwards, leaping two feet in the air from a standing four-footed start. Climbing Gran's curtains right to the top and then yowling from the curtain rail because they couldn't get down again. Gran had to rescue them twenty times a day.

"Why don't grown-up cats do those things?" asked David.

"Expect they can, but they see no need for it," said Gran. "Just as well. I don't think my curtains could take another set of kittens."

"They purr like little bees. And spit like little fireworks."

"Yes, they're almost ready to go. If only for Furble's sake." The she-cat, thin as a rail with huge burning eyes, called and called to the kittens who no longer took a blind bit of notice. She ran among them like a frantic teacher who has lost control of her class.

"They've got her worn out, poor love. They're adolescents now."

They taught them to drink milk, upending them and plunging their noses into the saucer. The kittens, released, would sneeze milk all over, then lick their noses with their tiny tongues.

"They'll soon get a taste for milk," said Gran. "Look at that greedy beggar, with all four feet in the saucer."

Later David helped rub cat food on their faces. They soon got the idea of that, too. Kittens got trodden on, sat on by the vicar when he called. You could not move for kittens. Whenever you sat down, they climbed up your legs in the most excruciating way.

Furble began to attack the kittens, throwing them down and biting them, scrabbling them with her back legs. Finally, the kittens made a fort under Gran's chair, and kept driving off their mother with fierce blows, whenever she came near. But when she tried to lie down to rest, they leapt fiercely and bit her tail.

"Time to go," said Gran.

David sat in the silent kitchen. Lucky and Romulus and Remus (re-named Ginger and Red) had gone to their good homes. Gran had taken Furble to the vet's to be spayed.

"I always like a she-cat to have one litter – it makes them nicer natured. But no more – there's far too many kittens in the world already."

Snowdrop lay in a chair, asleep. She had spent a lot of the morning wandering around, looking for the others and mewing sadly. She looked very small and grown-up and lonely as she lay asleep. David picked her up and put her on his knee and stroked her gently with one finger. It would never do to have Snowdrop turn into a dull, boring cat.

Like a tiny bee, Snowdrop began to purr.

It would be all right: just a lot of loving to do.

Tiger Story, Anansi Story

Philip Sherlock

1. Anansi Asks A Favour

Once upon a time, and a long, long time ago, all things were named after Tiger, for he was the strongest of all the animals, and King of the forest. The strong baboon, standing and smiting his chest like a drum, setting the trees ringing with his roars, respected Tiger and kept quiet before him. Even the brown monkey, so nimble and full of mischief, twisting the tail of the elephant, scampering about on the back of the sleeping alligator, pulling faces at the hippopotamus, even he was quiet before Tiger.

So, because Tiger ruled the forest, the lily whose flower bore red stripes was called tiger-lily, and the moth with broad, striped wings was called tiger-moth; and the stories that the animals told at evening in the forest were called Tiger Stories.

44

Of all the animals in the forest Anansi the spider was the weakest. One evening, looking up at Tiger, Anansi said, "Tiger, you are very strong. Everyone is quiet in your presence. You are King of the forest. I am not strong. No one pays any attention to me. Will you grant me a favour, O Tiger?"

The other animals began to laugh. How silly of feeble Anansi to be asking a favour of Tiger! The bullfrog gurgled and hurried off to the pond to tell his wife how silly Anansi was. The green parrot in the tree called to her brother to fly across and see what was happening.

But Tiger said nothing. He did not seem to know that Anansi had spoken to him. He lay quiet, head lifted, eyes half closed. Only the tip of his tail moved.

Anansi bowed low so that his forehead almost touched the ground. He stood in front of Tiger, but a little to one side, and said, "Good evening, Tiger. I have a favour to ask."

Tiger opened his eyes and looked at Anansi. He flicked his tail and asked, "What favour, Anansi?"

"Well," replied Anansi in his strange, lisping voice, "everything bears your name because you are strong. Nothing bears my name. Could something be called after me, Tiger? You have so many things named after you."

"What would you like to bear your name?" asked

Tiger, eyes half closed, tail moving slowly from side to side, his tawny, striped body quite still.

"The stories," replied Anansi. "Would you let them be called Anansi Stories?"

Now Tiger loved the stories, prizing them even more than the tiger-lily and the tiger-moth. Stupid Anansi, he thought to himself. Does he really think that I am going to permit these stories to be called Anansi Stories, after the weakest of all the animals in the forest? Anansi Stories indeed! He replied, "Very well, Anansi. Have your wish, have your wish, but . . ."

Tiger fell silent. All the animals listened. What did Tiger mean, agreeing to Anansi's request and then saying "but"? What trick was he up to? Parrot listened. Bullfrog stopped gurgling in order to catch the answer. Wise Owl, looking down from his hole in the trunk of a tree, waited for Tiger to speak.

"But what, Tiger? And it is so kind of you, Tiger, to do me this favour," cried Anansi.

"But," said Tiger, speaking loudly and slowly so that all might hear, "you must first do me two favours. Two favours from the weak equal one from the strong. Isn't that right, Anansi?"

"What two favours?" asked Anansi.

"You must first catch me a gourd full of live bees, Anansi. That is the first favour I ask of you."

At this all the animals laughed so loudly that Alligator came out of a nearby river to find out what was happening. How could weak Anansi catch a gourd full of bees? One or two sharp stings would put an end to that!

Anansi remained silent. Tiger went on, eyes half closed. "And there is a second favour that I ask, Anansi."

"What is that, Tiger?"

"Bring me Mr Snake alive. Mr Snake who lives down by the river, opposite the clump of bamboo-trees. Both these things you must do within seven days, Anansi. Do these two small things for me, and I will agree that the stories might be called after you. It was this you asked, wasn't it, Anansi?"

"Yes, Tiger," replied Anansi, "and I will do these two favours for you, as you ask."

"Good," replied Tiger. "I have often wished to sit and talk with Mr Snake. I have often wished to have my own hive of bees, Anansi. I am sure you will do what I ask. Do these two little things and you can have the stories."

Tiger leapt away suddenly through the forest, while the laughter of the animals rose in great waves of sound. How could Anansi catch live bees and a live snake? Anansi went off to his home, pursued by the laughter of Parrot and Bullfrog.

2. The First Task: A Gourd Full of Bees

On Monday morning Anansi woke early. He went into the woods, carrying an empty gourd, muttering to himself. "I wonder how many it can hold? I wonder how many it can hold?"

Ant asked him why he was carrying an empty gourd and talking to himself, but Anansi did not reply. Later, he met Iguana.

"What are you doing with the empty gourd?" asked Iguana. Anansi did not answer. Still further along the track he met a centipede walking along on his hundred legs.

"Why are you talking to yourself, Anansi?" asked Centipede, but Anansi made no reply.

Then Queen Bee flew by. She heard Centipede speaking to Anansi, and, full of curiosity, she asked, "Anansi, why are you carrying that empty gourd? Why are you talking to yourself?"

"Oh, Queen Bee," replied Anansi, "I have made a bet with Tiger, but I fear that I am going to lose. He bet me that I could not tell him how many bees a gourd can hold. Queen Bee, what shall I tell him?"

"Tell him it's a silly bet," replied Queen Bee.

"But you know how angry Tiger becomes, how quick-tempered he is," pleaded Anansi. "Surely you will help me?"

"I am not at all sure that I can," said Queen Bee as

she flew away. "How can I help you when I do not know myself how many bees it takes to fill an empty gourd?"

Anansi went back home with the gourd. In the afternoon he returned to the forest, making for the logwood-trees, which at this time of the year were heavy with sweet-smelling yellow flowers and full of the sound of bees. As he went along he kept saying aloud, "How many can it hold? How many can it hold?"

Centipede, who saw Anansi passing for the second time, told his friend Cricket that he was sure Anansi was out of his mind, for he was walking about in the forest asking himself the same question over and over again. Cricket sang the news to Bullfrog, and Bullfrog passed it on to Parrot, who reported it from his perch on the cedar-tree. Tiger heard and smiled to himself.

At about four o'clock that afternoon, Queen Bee, returning with her swarm of bees from the logwood-trees, met Anansi. He was still talking to himself. Well content with the work of the day, she took pity on him, and called out, "Wait there, Anansi. I have thought of a way of helping you."

"I am so glad, Queen Bee," said Anansi, "because I have been asking myself the same question all day and I cannot find the answer."

"Well," said Queen Bee, "all you have to do is measure one of my bees, then measure your empty gourd, divide one into the other and you will have the answer."

"But that's school-work, Queen Bee. I couldn't do that. I was never quick in school. That's too hard for me, too hard, Queen Bee. And that dreadful Tiger is so quick-tempered. What am I to do, Queen Bee?"

"I will tell you how to get the answer," said one of the bees that advised the Queen. "Really, it is quite easy. Hold the gourd with the opening towards the sunlight so that we can see it. We will fly in one at a time. You count us as we go in. When the gourd is full we will fly out. In this way you will find out the correct answer."

"Splendid," said Queen Bee. "What do you think of that, Anansi?"

"Certainly that will give the answer," replied Anansi, "and it will be more correct than the school answer. It is a good method, Queen Bee. See, I have the gourd ready, with the opening to the sunlight. Ready?"

Slowly the bees flew in, their Queen leading the way, with Anansi counting, "One, two, three, four, five . . . twenty-one, twenty-two, twenty-three . . . forty-one, forty-two, forty-three, forty-four," until the gourd was half full, three-quarters full, ". . . a

hundred and fifty-two, and fifty-three, and fifty-four."
At that point the last bee flew in, filling the gourd,
now heavy with humming bees crowded together.
Anansi corked up the opening and hurried off to the
clearing in the forest where Tiger sat with a circle of
animals.

"See, King Tiger," he said, "here is your gourd full
of bees, one hundred and fifty-four of them, all full of
logwood honey. Do you still want me to bring
Brother Snake, or is this enough?"

Tiger was so angry that he could hardly restrain
himself from leaping at Anansi and tearing him to
pieces. He had been laughing with the other animals

at Parrot's account of Anansi walking alone through the forest asking himself the same ridiculous question over and over. Tiger was pleased about one thing only, that he had set Anansi two tasks and not one. Well, he had brought the gourd full of bees. But one things was certain. He could never bring Mr Snake alive.

"What a good thing it is that I am so clever," said Tiger to himself. "If I had set him only one task I would have lost the stories." Feeling more content within himself, and proud of his cleverness, he replied to Anansi, who was bowing low before him, "Of course, Anansi. I set you one thing that I knew you could do, and one that I know you cannot do. It's Monday evening. You have until Saturday morning, so hurry off and be gone with you."

The animals laughed while Anansi limped away. He always walked like that, resting more heavily on one leg than on the others. All laughed, except Wise Owl, looking down from his home in the cedar-tree. The strongest had set the weakest two tasks.

Perhaps, thought Owl to himself, perhaps . . . perhaps . . .

3. The Second Task: Mr Snake

On Tuesday morning Anansi got up early. How was he to catch Mr Snake? The question had been buzzing about in his head all night, like an angry wasp. How to catch Mr Snake?

Perhaps he could trap Snake with some ripe bananas. He would make a Calaban beside the path that Snake used each day when the sky beat down on the forest and he went to the stream to quench his thirst. How good a thing it is, thought Anansi, that Snake is a man of such fixed habits; he wakes up at the same hour each morning, goes for his drink of water at the same hour, hunts for his food every afternoon, goes to bed at sunset each day.

Anansi worked hard making his Calaban to catch Snake. He took a vine, pliant yet strong, and made a noose in it. He spread grass and leaves over the vine to hide it. Inside the noose he placed two ripe bananas. When Snake touched the noose, Anansi would draw it tight. How angry Mr Snake would be, to find that he had been trapped! Anansi smiled to himself while he put the finishing touches to the trap, then he hid himself in the bush by the side of the track, holding one end of the vine.

Anansi waited quietly. Not a leaf stirred. Lizard was asleep on the trunk of a tree opposite. Looking down the path Anansi could see heat waves rising from the parched ground.

There was Snake, his body moving quietly over the grass and dust, a long gleaming ribbon marked in green and brown. Anansi waited. Snake saw the bananas and moved towards them. He lay across the vine and ate the bananas. Anansi pulled at the vine to tighten the noose, but Snake's body was too heavy. When he had eaten the bananas Snake went on his way to the stream.

That was on Tuesday. Anansi returned home, the question still buzzing about in his head: "How to catch Snake? How to catch Snake?" When his wife asked him what he would like for supper, he answered, "How to catch Snake?" When his son asked if he could go off for a game with his cousin, Anansi replied, "How to catch Snake?"

A Slippery Hole! That was the answer. Early on Wednesday morning he hurried back to the path in the forest where he had waited for Snake the day before, taking with him a ripe avocado pear. Snake liked avocado pears better even than bananas. In the middle of the path Anansi dug a deep hole, and made the sides slippery with grease. At the bottom he put the pear. If Snake went down into the hole he would not be able to climb back up the slippery sides. Then Anansi hid in the bush.

At noon Snake came down the path. "How long he is," said Anansi to himself, "long and strong. Will I ever be able to catch him?"

Snake glided down the path, moving effortlessly

until he came to the Slippery Hole. He looked over the edge of the hole and saw the avocado pear at the bottom. Also he saw that the sides of the hole were slippery. First he wrapped his tail tightly round the trunk of a slender tree beside the track, then lowered his body and ate the avocado pear. When he had finished he pulled himself out of the hole by his tail and went on his way to the river. Anansi had lost the bananas; now he had lost the avocado pear also!

On Wednesday Anansi spent the morning working at a "Fly-Up", a trap he had planned during the night while the question buzzed through his head: "How to catch Snake. How? How?" He arranged it cleverly, fitting one of the slender young bamboo-trees with a noose, so that the bamboo flew up at the slightest touch, pulling the noose tight. Inside the noose he put an egg, the only one that he had left. It was precious to him, but he knew that Snake loved eggs even more than he did. Then he waited behind the clump of bamboos. Snake came down the path.

The Fly-Up did not catch Snake, who simply lowered his head, took the egg up in his mouth without touching the noose, and then enjoyed the egg in the shade of the clump of bamboos while Anansi looked on. He had lost the bananas and avocado pear, and his precious egg.

There was nothing more to do. The question "How

to catch Snake?" no longer buzzed round and round in his head, keeping him awake by night, troubling him throughout the day. The Calaban, the Slippery Hole and the Fly-Up had failed. He would have to go back to Tiger and confess that he could not catch Snake. How Parrot would laugh, and Bullfrog and Monkey!

Friday came. Anansi did nothing. There was no more that he could do.

Early on Saturday morning, before daybreak, Anansi set off for a walk by the river, taking his cutlass with him. He passed by the hole where Snake lived. Snake was up early. He was looking towards the east, waiting for the sun to rise, his head resting on the edge of his hole, his long body hidden in the earth. Anansi had not expected that Snake would be up so early. He had forgotten Snake's habit of rising early to see the dawn. Remembering how he had tried to catch Snake, he went by very quietly, limping a little, hoping that Snake would not notice him. But Snake did.

"You there, you, Anansi, stop there!" called Snake.

"Good morning, Snake," replied Anansi. "How angry you sound."

"And angry I am," said Snake. "I have a good mind to eat you for breakfast." Snake pulled half his body out of the hole. "You have been trying to catch me.

You set a trap on Monday, a Calaban. Lizard told me.
You thought he was asleep on the trunk of the tree
but he was not; and as you know, we are of the same
family. And on Tuesday you set a Slippery Hole, and
on Wednesday a Fly-Up. I have a good mind to kill
you, Anansi."

"Oh, Snake, I beg your pardon. I beg your pardon,"
cried the terrified Anansi. "What you say is true. I
did try to catch you, but I failed. You are too clever
for me."

"And why did you try to catch me, Anansi?"

"I had a bet with Tiger. I told him you are the
longest animal in the world, even longer than that
long bamboo-tree by the side of the river."

"Of course I am," shouted Snake. "Of course I am.
You haven't got to catch me to prove that. Of course
I am longer than the bamboo-tree!" At this, Snake,
who was now very angry and excited, drew his body
out of the hole and stretched himself out on the
grass. "Look!" he shouted. "Look! How dare Tiger
say that the bamboo-tree is longer than I am!"

"Well," said Anansi, "you are very long, very long
indeed. But, Snake, now that I see you and the
bamboo-tree at the same time, it seems to me that the
bamboo-tree is a little longer than you are; just a few
inches longer, Snake, half a foot or a foot at the most.
Oh, Snake, I have lost my bet. Tiger wins!"

"Tiger, fiddlesticks!" shouted the enraged Snake. "Anyone can see that the bamboo-tree is shorter than I am. Cut it down, you stupid creature! Put it beside me. Measure the bamboo-tree against my body. You haven't lost your bet, you have won."

Anansi hurried off to the clump of bamboos, cut down the longest and trimmed off the branches.

"Now put it beside me," shouted the impatient Snake.

Anansi put the long bamboo pole beside Snake. Then he said, "Snake, you are very long, very long indeed. But we must go about this in the correct way. Perhaps when I run up to your head you will crawl up, and when I run down to see where your tail is you will wriggle down. How I wish I had someone to help me measure you with the bamboo!"

"Tie my tail to the bamboo," said Snake, "and get on with the job. You can see that I am longer!"

Anansi tied Snake's tail to one end of the bamboo. Running up to the other end, he called, "Now stretch, Snake, stretch!"

Snake stretched as hard he could. Turtle, hearing the shouting, came out of the river to see what was happening. A flock of white herons flew across the river, and joined in, shouting, "Stretch, Snake, stretch." It was more exciting than a race. Snake was stretching his body to its utmost, but the bamboo was some inches longer.

"Good," cried Anansi. "I will tie you round the middle, Snake, then you can try again. One more try, and you will prove you are longer than the bamboo."

Anansi tied Snake to the bamboo, round the middle. Then he said, "Now rest for five minutes. When I shout, 'Stretch', then stretch as much as you can."

"Yes," said one of the herons. "You have only six inches to stretch, Snake. You can do it."

Snake rested for five minutes. Anansi shouted, "Stretch." Snake made a mighty effort. The herons and Turtle cheered Snake on. He shut his eyes for the last tremendous effort that would prove him longer than the bamboo.

"Hooray," shouted the animals, "you are winning, you are winning, four inches more, two inches more . . ."

At that moment Anansi tied Snake's head to the bamboo. The animals fell silent. There was Snake tied to the bamboo, ready to be taken to Tiger.

From that day the stories have been called Anansi Stories.

A Grave Misunderstanding

Leon Garfield

I am a dog. I think you ought to know right away. I don't want to save it up for later, because you might begin to wonder what sort of a person it was who went about on all fours, sniffing at bottoms and peeing up against lamp-posts in the public street. You wouldn't like it; and I don't suppose you'd care to have anything more to do with me.

The truth of the matter is, we have different standards, me and my colleagues, that is; not in everything, I hasten to bark, but in enough for it to be noticeable. For instance, although we are as fond of a good walk as the next person, love puppies and smoked salmon, we don't go much on reading. We find it hard to turn the pages. But, on the other paw, a good deep snoutful of mingled air as it comes humming off a rubbish dump can be as teasing to us as a sonnet. Indeed, there are rhymes in rancid odours such as you'd never dream of; and every puddle tells a story.

We see things, too. Only the other day, when me and my Person were out walking, and going as brisk as biscuits, through the green and quiet place of marble trees and stony, lightless lamp-posts, where people bury their bones and never dig them up, I saw a ghost. I stopped. I glared, I growled, my hair stood on end –

"What the devil's the matter with you now?" demanded my Person.

"What a beautiful dog!" said the ghost, who knew that I knew what she was, and that we both knew that my Person did not.

She was the lifeless, meaningless shell of a young female person whose bones lay not very far away. No heart beat within her, there was wind in her veins, and she smelled of worm-crumble and pine.

"Thank you," said my Person, with a foolishly desiring smile: for the ghost's eyes were very come-hitherish, even though her hither was thither, under the grass. "He *is* rather a handsome animal. Best of breed at Cruft's you know." The way to his heart was always open through praise of me.

"Does he bite?" asked the ghost, watching me with all the empty care of nothingness trying to be something.

"SHE'S DEAD – SHE'S DEAD!"

"Stop barking!" said my Person. "Don't be frightened. He wouldn't hurt a fly. Do you come here often?"

"Every day," murmured the ghost, with a sly look towards her bones. She moved a little nearer to my Person. A breeze sprang up, and I could smell it blowing right through her, like frozen flowers. "He looks very fierce," said the ghost. "Are you sure that he's kind?"

"COME AWAY – COME AWAY!"

"Stop barking!" commanded my Person, and looked at the ghost with springtime in his eyes. If only he could have smelled the dust inside her head, and heard the silence inside her breast! But it was no good. All he could see was a silken smile. He was only a person, and blindly trusted his eyes . . .

"Dogs," said the ghost, "should be kept on a lead in the churchyard. There's a notice on the gate." She knew that I knew where she was buried, and that I'd just been going to dig up her bones.

My Person obeyed; and the ghost looked at me as if to say, "Now you'll never be able to show him that I'm dead!"

"SHE'S COLD! SHE'S EMPTY! SHE'S GRAND-DAUGHTER DEATH!"

"Stop barking!" shouted my Person, and, dragging me after, walked on, already half in love with the loveless ghost.

We passed very close to her bones. I could smell them, and I could hear the little nibblers dryly rustling. I pulled, I strained, I jerked to dig up her secret . . .

"He looks so wild!" said the ghost. "His eyes are rolling and his jaws are dripping. Are you sure he doesn't have a fever? Don't you think he ought to go to the vet?"

"He only wants to run off and play," said my Person. "Do you live near here?"

"YES! YES! RIGHT BY THAT MARBLE LAMP-POST! SIX PAWS DEEP IN THE EARTH!"

"Stop barking!" said my Person. "Do you want to wake up the dead?"

The ghost started. Then she laughed, like the wind among rotting leaves. "I have a room nearby," she murmured. "A little room all to myself. It is very convenient, you know."

"A little room all to yourself?" repeated my Person, his heart beating with eager concern. "How lonely that must be!"

"Yes," she said. "Sometimes it is very lonely in my little room, even though I hear people walking and talking upstairs, over my head."

"Then let me walk back with you," said my Person, "and keep you company."

"No dogs allowed," said the ghost. "They would turn me out, you know."

"Then come my way!" said my Person; and the ghost raised her imitation eyebrows in imitation surprise. "Madam, will you walk," sang my Person laughingly. "Madam, will you talk, Madam, will you walk and talk with me?"

"I don't see why not," smiled the ghost.

"BECAUSE SHE'S DEAD – DEAD – DEAD!"

"Stop barking!" said my Person. " 'I will give you the keys of Heaven, I will give you the keys of my heart . . .' "

"The keys of Heaven?" sighed the ghost. "Would you really?"

"And the keys of my heart! Will you have dinner with me?"

"Are you inviting me into your home?"

"NO GHOSTS ALLOWED! SHE'LL TURN ME OUT!"

"Stop barking! Yes . . . if you'd like to!"

"Oh I would indeed – I would indeed!"

"DON'T DO IT! YOU'LL BE BRINGING DEATH INTO OUR HOME!"

"For God's sake, stop that barking! This way . . . this way . . ."

It was hopeless, hopeless! There was only one

thing left for a dog to do. *She* knew what it was, of course: she could see it in my eyes. She walked on the other side of my Person, and always kept him between herself and me. I bided my time . . .

"Do you like Italian food?" asked my Person.

"Not spaghetti," murmured the ghost. "It reminds me of worms."

It was then that I broke free. I jerked forward with all my strength and wrenched the lead from out of my Person's grasp. He shouted! The ghost glared and shrank away. For a moment I stared into her eyes, and she stared into mine.

"Dogs must be kept on a lead!" whispered the ghost as I jumped. "There's a notice on . . . on . . . on . . ."

It was like jumping through cobwebs and feathers; and when I turned, she'd vanished like a puff of air. I saw the grass shiver, and I knew she'd gone back to her bones.

"SHE WAS DEAD! SHE WAS DEAD! I TOLD YOU SO!"

My Person didn't answer. He was shaking, he was trembling; for the very first time, he couldn't believe his eyes.

"What happened? Where – where is she? Where has she gone?"

I showed him. Trailing my lead, I went to where she lay, six paws under, and began to dig.

"No! No!" he shrieked. "For God's sake, let her lie there in peace!"

Thankfully I stopped. The earth under the grass was thick and heavy, and the going was hard. I went back to my Person. He had collapsed on a bench and was holding his head in his hands. I tried to comfort him by licking his ear.

A female person walked neatly by. She was young and smooth and shining, and smelled of coffee and cats. She was dressed in the softest of white.

"Oh, what a beautiful dog," she said, pausing to admire me.

He stared up at her. His eyes widened; his teeth began to chatter. He could not speak.

"GO ON! GO ON! 'BEST OF BREED AT CRUFT'S!'"

"Hush!" said the female person, reproaching me with a gentle smile. "You'll wake up the dead!"

"Is she real?" whispered my Person, his eyes as wide and round as tins. "Or is she a ghost? Show me, show me! Try to jump through her like you did before! Jump, jump!"

"BUT SHE'S REAL! SHE'S ALIVE!"

"Stop barking and jump!"

So I jumped. She screamed – but not in fright. She screamed with rage. My paws were still thick and filthy with churchyard mud, and, in a moment, so was her dress.

"You – you madman!" she shouted at my shame-faced Person. "You told him to do it! You told him to jump! You're not fit to have a dog!"

"But – but—" he cried out as she stormed away, to report him, she promised, to the churchyard authorities and the RSPCA.

"I TOLD YOU SHE WAS ALIVE! I TOLD YOU SO!"

"Stop barking!" wept my Person. "Please!"

A Bit of Bread and Jam

Bill Naughton

It was one o'clock on Saturday afternoon, and eleven of us boys were setting out from our street to go fishing. Suddenly the woman at the end house, whose name was Mrs Hoskey, bobbed her head out of the door and called out to us.

"Hy, will one of you boys go on an errand for me?"

We none of us answered. We all knew her. She was one of those women who liked to have you mugging around for an hour, and would then promise you a penny, which you never got.

"Hy," she called again after us.

"Don't go," whispered Felix Stringfellow. "It's not worth it. She'll send you to the tripe shop for some trotters, to Clarke's for some toffees, to the paper-shop for some love books, an' when you've worn your shoe-leather away, she'll give you a miserable bit of bread an' jam."

"A rotten jam butty," said Sammy Feathers.

Felix was in our gang, and we none of us went against him. He had turned fifteen and was already working in the factory.

"Why don't you send Albert?" he called, with a beckon of his thumb at little Mr Hoskey, who was pegging out washing in the back street.

"He's busy," she said. Then she caught my eye. "Hy, you, Billy – you'll not see me stuck?"

She was a big fat woman with red hair, and I'd once heard somebody say she could put the evil eye on you. I didn't want that happening when I was going off fishing.

"I'll not be long, lads," I said.

"Gaa," snorted Felix, "a fat lot you'll get." And off he went with the gang.

He was right about that errand, except that she had a quarter-pound of snuff as well. And he was dead right about the jam butty.

"There's a nice bit of our Albert's bakin'" she said, wrapping it up in paper and trying to make it look a lot.

"You can't give that to young Billy, Ada," cried Albert. "I tell you it didn't rise properly."

"If you poke your nose into my business," she said to him, "I'll put you up the chimney. S'help me."

Little Albert looked uncomfortable and unhappy. "But it hasn't risen," he said. Then he looked at me as though he was going to burst out crying, "Billy, don't eat it!" At that his wife let out one roar, and I went off with my jam butty.

One bite convinced me that his advice was sound. I chewed it for a hundred yards or so, just to give it a chance. But then I marked one of those wide sewer grids along the street, and I dropped the mouthful down. Then I ran to Pike's Lodge.

Every inch of the muddy bank was thronged with kids of all ages, fishing away with all their might. There was a din of argument going on, the constant *perlop* of a worm on a pin hitting the water, and the excited *perluff* of a writhing stickleback being pulled out. I raced up the bank, kicked up a sod of grass with the toe of my clog, pawed madly into the soil, grabbed a worm, and, unreeling my line at the same time, I hurried off to my own gang.

Felix was up to his shins in mud, and held a line in each hand. Beside him was a great big toffee tin that was already heaving with fish. Just as I forced my way in beside him he drew in both lines.

"Seven!" I yelled, seeing them wriggling in the sunshine. "Four red doctors among 'em."

Instead of slipping them off, Felix looked at them with a sour face, and even stood watching while two got away.

"Have you gone daft?" I said.

"There's nowt to it," said Felix. "I'm fed up to the eye tooth." He looked round at the mob. "You throw in an' they're on before the worm hits the water. It aren't fishin' – it's mass suicide. Even wenches are catchin' 'em." Then he picked up the can in both hands and flung all the fish back in.

We could hardly believe our own eyes. Not that I felt so bad, because I hadn't caught any.

"There's nowt to it," said Felix.

"What's on your mind?" said Sammy Feathers.

"I want to do summat as needs a bit of doin'," said Felix. "Such as catching a carp. A carp aren't like a stickleback – it don't bite."

"What does it do?" I said.

"*Ssucks*," said Felix. "A carp gives a suck at the bait to see if it likes it. The float does no more than tremble. Then tha strikes. That's what I call fishin'."

"But where can we catch carp, Felix?"

"Our mill lodge."

"Pratt an' Dyson's?" said Sammy. "Not a chance!"

"Why? The watchman?"

"No, the *carp*. Our old chap has fished every lodge, lake, an' canal in the British Isles, an' he reckons there's no fish in this wide world wants as much catching as one of Pratt an' Dyson's carp. They're that pampered that they don't even suck."

"What do they do?"

"*Sniff*. They just sniff the bait – an' you gotta strike then."

"That sort of fishing," said Felix. "I'd say there was summat to."

"Aye, but nobody ever catches any."

"You don't have to tell me," said Felix. "I work there. Come on, chaps."

We all followed him to the back of Pratt and Dyson's mill. A very high fence with a barbed wire top surrounded the mill lodge. "The watchman has his tea from four to half past," said Felix. "He's as deaf as a doornail an' can't see a yard in front of him, so don't worry."

I saw a knot-hole in the wood and I peeped through. "No use, there's one chap fishing."

Felix shoved me out of the way and had a look for himself. "It's our managing director," he said. "Charlie Pratt. Come on, give me a cock up, an' I'll see what he says." We gave him a leg up, and he got his head over the top. "'Lo, Mister Pratt! I work in number seven room under Alec Ackers. Would it be all right if me an' my mates had a quiet ten minutes with you?"

"It will be quiet," we heard him say. "I've been here since early morning an' never had a stir. But if you can get in, you're welcome to it. Don't say I gave you permission."

"OK, lads," said Felix, "he says we can go in." Then he hurried along the boards, tapping each one. "There's a false 'un, if I can find it. Ah, here it is." A slat of wood gave way, and Felix crept in, we all followed, and he replaced it. For a minute none of us spoke. It was as though we had entered some wonderful land, after all the din and mud of the Pike Lodge. Here it was beautifully quiet, everything spotless; the water was pale green, and the fat, lazy carp, some a lovely red and gold, were gliding about in the depth.

We began to feel about in our pockets for hooks and catgut. "Oh, but what about bait?" exclaimed Sammy Feathers.

"Crikey, these won't look at worms," said Felix. "We need some good dough."

"You can divide this bit up, lads," said Mr Pratt. "I've just about had enough."

There was a rush for the ball of bait. Before I could get there it was all gone. "Hy, what about me?" I said.

"*Sh, sh*," whispered Felix. "I hope we're not driving you away, Mister Pratt?"

"Ten hours, laddie," he said, "without a bite, is enough even for me." He began to pack up his fishing gear slowly.

In no time they all had their lines on the go. And there I was without a crumb of bait for mine. I went mooching away to a corner to sulk. Then suddenly,

I felt the remnant of the jam butty in my pocket. I turned away from the others, got it out and, unable to separate the bread from the jam, I put the lot in my hanky, kneaded it up, adding drops of spittle to make it doughy. I took a peck between finger and thumb, rolled it into a pellet, carefully pressed it on to my hook, made myself comfortable, looked at the water, then softly cast in.

Suddenly my float disappeared. *What's up?* I thought. *What's up? Where's it gone?* I half pulled it out, felt something there, and struck. Up came my line out of the water Wriggling and twittering at the end of it was a lovely fat carp!

Flummoxed for a second or two, I could do no more than stare at it and think: *Is this happening to me?* And then I heard Felix give a shout, "Quick, som'dy, where's can?" I turned and saw them all staring open-gobbed at me. I swung the line in, and by luck my left hand grasped the fish first time. It felt as thick as a fat polony sausage and full of life. Some power came to my fingers and extricated the hook. With my left hand I held the fish under water, not even bothering to look down at it, and as Felix spluttered to get the can filled with water I remarked casually, "What's all the fuss about, man? Tak' your time."

I rolled another pellet of bait, while a cluster of heads was over the tin. As I cast in again, heard the pleasant *ping* of the tiny weights striking the water surface, I felt a relaxed calm coming to me. Then I gave a jump as there was a cry from Felix: "you're under!"

I gave a jerk. The gleam of a carp in the air, jiggling the next instant on the bank. I just blurted out, "Tak' it off, Felix." Eagerly he obeyed. I kept my face down. It didn't feel like it belonged to me. But I had wits enough to stick the hanky bait down in my pocket. Little Albert's baking, I thought, worth a fortune.

In no time they had crowded my pitch. Not a single bite, however, but mine. I missed three, and moved farther along the bank. Mr Pratt gave me a begging look, and I slipped him a morsel of bait. He landed two beauties in about five minutes. As for me, I was catching them and missing them every other minute.

"*Sniff?*" remarked Felix to Sammy. "They're biting like tiger sharks, tell your father. Hy, we've just a round dozen – what about getting another can?"

But the watchman arrived just then. "You might be the boss during the week," he said to Mr Pratt, "but I'm in charge over the weekend. I'm not having it."

I was glad to get away, for the strain was telling.

"You can all have one apiece," I said, feeling generous, "an' I'll have two." The secret of the bait I didn't share, even turning down a bribe from Mr Pratt. With carp fetching fourpence each, and gold ones a tanner, I reckoned I'd make a fortune over the season. All I had to do was play my cards right with little Albert and the watchman.

"I say, chaps," said Felix, as we turned the street corner, "what's everybody out for? What are they all chunnering about? Look, Bill, the ambulance is outside your door."

At that moment Felix's mother spotted me and let out a yell: "He's here! He's here!"

Out came my mother, running to me, with a policeman beside her. "Are you all right, love?" she screamed, putting her arms round me.

I shoved her off. "Let go! 'Course I am."

Then the policeman calmed her down. "He'll be all right, ma." He turned to me. "Are you the lad that had the jam butty given you by Mrs Hoskey at the end house at half past one today?"

"Aye, I am."

"How do you feel?"

"Champion. Leastways, I did."

"Come on, laddie," he said, patting me on the head, "in the ambulance."

"What for? Like this?"

"Aye, there's no time to dress up. Keep calm, ma," he said, helping my mother in.

"What's up, Mum?" I heard Felix ask.

"Little Albert," she said, "bashed Ada on the napper with a mallet."

"About time somebody did."

"Only stunned her."

"Pity!"

"That's why he gave himself up – to get safely out of her way."

The driver shut the white ambulance door.

"When did you eat it, sonny?" asked the attendant as we moved off.

"Eat what?"

"The jam butty."

They were gazing at me pitifully, and my mother was crying her eyes out.

"I didn't."

"What?" yelled the attendant, rapping on the panel. "Stop!"

"What did you do with it?" asked the policeman.

I thought for a minute before answering. I pictured all the carp I was going to catch. "The first grid I came to," I said, "I put it down."

"Oh, I'll warm you, my lad," cried my mother, grabbing me by the shoulders, "for givin' us all such a fright."

"You'll be all right now, ma." The policeman opened the door and let her out. "I'll have him home with you in ten minutes." Then he turned to the attendant. "Drop us off at the town hall – our inspector wants a word with the lad."

Into the police inspector's office I went, and all my words were taken down in writing.

"Tell the prisoner to stop worrying about the lad," said the inspector to a jailer. "Tell him he never ate it."

As the policeman was taking me back to the tram I said to him, "What's all this fuss about a jam butty?"

"It were *dosed*," he stooped and whispered in my ear, "dosed heavy."

"Whatever with?"

"*Arsenic!*"

For a moment I had to put my hand against the wall just to steady my knees.

"Enough," went on the policeman, "to kill a regiment. It were all the top off the jam – where he'd planted it for her. An' the bread itself were fair weighted wi' it. Don't breathe a word, lad, but it's God's mercy you're not stretched stone stiff in the morgue this very minute."

When I reached the street corner I was suddenly confronted by Felix.

"Hy, know what? Know what, Bill?" he cried in alarm. "The fish, every bloomin' one swimmin' round like mad, swellin' up an' dropping stone stiff dead!"

Seeing him so upset over a few paltry carp caused a strange calm to come over me. "Felix," I said, putting a hand on his shoulder, "forget it. There's nowt to it."

Leaving him staring flabbergasted at me, I staggered lightly up the street, neither knowing nor caring whether they'd fuss me at home, or give me a right good hiding.

The Grey Cub

Jack London

He was different from his brothers and sisters. Their hair already betrayed the reddish hue inherited from their mother, the she-wolf; while he alone, in this particular, took after his father. He was the one little grey cub of the litter. He had bred true to the straight wolf-stock – in fact, he had bred true to old One Eye himself, physically, with but a single exception, and that was – he had two eyes to his father's one.

The grey cub's eyes had not been open long, yet already he could see with steady clearness. And while his eyes were still closed, he had felt, tasted, and smelled. He knew his two brothers and his two sisters very well. He had begun to romp with them in a feeble, awkward way, and even to squabble, his little throat vibrating with a queer rasping noise (the forerunner of the growl), as he worked himself into a passion. And long before his eyes had opened, he had learned by touch, taste, and smell to know his mother – a fount of warmth and liquid food and tenderness. She possessed a gentle, caressing tongue that soothed him when it passed over his soft little body, and that impelled him to snuggle against her and to doze off to sleep.

Most of the first month of his life had been passed thus in sleeping; but now he could see quite well, and he stayed awake for longer periods of time, and he was coming to learn his world quite well. His world was gloomy; but he did not know that, for he knew no other world. It was dim-lighted; but his eyes had never had to adjust themselves to any other light. His world was very small. Its limits were the walls of the lair; but as he had no knowledge of the wide world outside, he was never oppressed by the narrow confines of his existence.

But he had early discovered that one wall of his world was different from the rest. This was the mouth of the cave and the source of light. He had discovered that it was different from the other walls long before he had any thoughts of his own, any conscious volitions. It had been an irresistible attraction before ever his eyes opened and looked upon it. The light from it had beat upon his sealed lids, and the eyes and the optic nerves had pulsated to little, spark-like flashes, warm-coloured and strangely pleasing. The life of his body and of every fibre of his body, the life that was the very substance of his body and that was apart from his own personal life, had yearned towards this light, and urged his body towards it in the same way that the cunning chemistry of a plant urges it towards the sun.

Always, as in the beginning, before his conscious life dawned, he had crawled towards the mouth of the cave. And in this his brothers and sisters were one with him. Never, in that period, did any of them crawl towards the dark corners of the back wall. The light drew them as if they were plants; the chemistry of the life that composed them demanded the light as a necessity of being; and their little puppet-bodies crawled blindly and chemically, like the tendrils of a vine. Later on, when each developed individuality and became personally conscious of impulsions and desires, the attraction of the light increased. They were always crawling and sprawling towards it, and being driven back from it by their mother.

It was in this way that the grey cub learned other attributes of his mother than the soft, soothing tongue. In his insistent crawling towards the light, he discovered in her a nose that with a sharp nudge administered rebuke, and later, a paw, that crushed him down and rolled him over and over with a swift, calculating stroke. Thus he learned hurt; and on top of it he learned to avoid hurt – first, by not incurring the risk of it; and second, when he had incurred the risk, by dodging and by retreating. These were conscious actions, and were the results of his first generalizations upon the world. Before that he had recoiled automatically from hurt, as he had crawled automatically towards the light. After that he had recoiled from hurt because he *knew* that it was hurt.

He was a fierce little cub. So were his brothers and sisters. It was to be expected. He was a carnivorous animal. He came of a breed of meat-killers and meat-eaters. His father and mother lived wholly upon meat. The milk he had sucked with his first flickering life was milk transformed directly from meat; and now, at a month old, when his eyes had been open for about a week, he was beginning himself to eat meat – meat half digested by the she-wolf and disgorged for the five growing cubs that already made too great a demand upon her breast.

But he was, further, the fiercest of the litter. He could make a louder rasping growl than any of them. His tiny rages were much more terrible than theirs. It was he that first learned the trick of rolling a fellow-cub over with a cunning paw-stroke. And it was he that first gripped another cub by the ear and pulled and tugged and growled through jaws tight-clenched. And certainly it was he that caused the mother the most trouble in keeping her litter from the mouth of the cave.

The fascination of the light for the grey cub increased from day to day. He was perpetually departing on yard-long adventures towards the cave's entrance, and as perpetually being driven back. Only he did not know it for an entrance. He did not know anything about entrances – passages whereby one goes from one place to another place. He did not know any other place, much less of a way to get there. So to him the entrance of the cave was a wall – a wall of light. As the sun was to the outside dweller, this was to him the sun of his world. It attracted him as a candle attracts a moth. He was always striving to attain it. The life that was so swiftly expanding within him urged him continually towards the wall of light. The life that was within him knew that it was the one way out, the way he was predestined to tread. But he himself did not know anything about it. He did not know there was any outside at all.

There was one strange thing about this wall of light. His father (he had already come to recognize his father as the one other dweller in the world, a creature like his mother, who slept near the light and was a bringer of meat) – his father had a way of walking right into the white far wall and

disappearing. The grey cub could not understand this. Though never permitted by his mother to approach that wall, he had approached the other walls, and encountered hard obstruction on the end of his tender nose. This hurt. And after several such adventures, he left the walls alone. Without thinking about it, he accepted this disappearing into the wall as a peculiarity of his father, as milk and half-digested meat were peculiarities of his mother.

In fact, the grey cub was not given to thinking – at least, to the kind of thinking customary of men. His brain worked in dim ways. Yet his conclusions were as sharp and distinct as those achieved by men. He had a method of accepting things without questioning the way and wherefore. In reality, this was the act of classification. He was never disturbed over *why* a thing happened. *How* it happened was sufficient for him. Thus, when he had bumped his nose on the back wall a few times, he accepted that he would not disappear into walls. In the same way he accepted that his father could disappear into walls. But he was not in the least disturbed by desire to find out the reason for the difference between his father and himself. Logic and physics were no part of his mental make-up.

Like most creatures of the Wild, he early experienced famine. There came a time when not only did the meat-supply cease, but the milk no longer came from his mother's breast. At first, the cubs whimpered and cried, but for the most part they slept. It was not long before they were reduced to a coma of hunger. There were no more spats and squabbles, no more tiny rages nor attempts at growling; while the adventures towards the far white wall ceased altogether. The cubs slept, while the life that was in them flickered and died down.

One Eye was desperate. He ranged far and wide, and slept but little in the lair that had now become cheerless and miserable. The she-wolf, too, left her litter and went out in search of meat. In the first days after the birth of the cubs, One Eye had journeyed several times back to the Indian camp and robbed the rabbit snares, but, with the melting of the snow and the opening of the streams, the Indian camp had moved away, and that source of supply was closed to him.

When the grey cub came back to life and again took interest in the far white wall, he found that the population of his world had been reduced. Only one sister remained to him. The rest were gone. As he grew stronger, he found himself compelled to play alone, for the sister no longer lifted her head nor moved about. His little body rounded out with the meat he now ate; but the food had come too late for her. She slept continuously, a tiny skeleton flung round with skin in which the flame flickered lower and lower and at last went out.

Then there came a time when the grey cub no longer saw his father appearing and disappearing in the wall, nor lying down asleep in the entrance. This had happened at the end of a second and less severe famine. The she-wolf knew why One Eye never came back, but there was no way by which she could tell what she had seen to the grey cub. Hunting herself for meat, up the left fork of the stream where lived the lynx, she had followed a day-old trail of One Eye. And she had found him, or what remained of him, at the end of the trail. There were many signs of the battle that had been fought, and of the lynx's withdrawal to her lair after having won the victory. Before she went away, the she-wolf had found this lair, but the signs told her that the lynx was inside, and she had not dared to venture in.

After that, the she-wolf in her hunting avoided the left fork. For she knew that in the lynx's lair was a litter of kittens, and she knew the lynx for a fierce, bad-tempered creature and a terrible fighter. It was all very well for half a dozen wolves to drive a lynx, spitting and bristling, up a tree; but it was quite a different matter for a lone wolf to encounter a lynx – especially when the lynx was known to have a litter of hungry kittens at her back.

But the Wild is the Wild, and motherhood is motherhood, at all times fiercely protective, whether in the wild or out of it; and the time was to come when the she-wolf, for her grey cub's sake would venture the left fork, and the lair in the rocks, and the lynx's wrath.

The Broken Bridge

Reginald Ottley

The rain roared down – great driving sheets of it, that rattled the corrugated iron.

Hunched over a table in the rough Bush hut, I knew I had to make a decision. If the rain kept on much longer, as well it might, I could be stranded for weeks. Yet if I left immediately, I had no way of knowing how much flood damage had already been done; though I did know I would get a cold, sodden soaking.

At last I said, "Well, it's not gettin' any easier. This is the third day now, an' you'll soon be out of tucker. Besides, I'd better get that mare home."

Bill, the boundary rider whose hut it was, nodded. He was a big quiet man who had offered me shelter when the rain started.

"Yeah," he said. "If that's how you see it. I don't mind the tucker, but the other's up to you."

I agreed that it was, and rolled my blankets.

Outside in the teeming rain I strapped them to my saddle. Then I humped the whole – saddle, bridle and blanket roll – over to the horse-yards. In one of them stood Midnight, my saddle-horse. In another was the brood mare I was leading home from a distant property. She was heavy in foal, and could give birth any time. A previously injured leg, now healed, had stopped her from being taken home sooner.

As I saddled Midnight, he stood staring beyond me to the brood mare. Maybe he sensed something – I don't know. He was a strange horse; bad, some would have called him. I had broken him some weeks before, but he had never accepted the breaking. Oh yes, I could ride and steer him, though never without a fight. Yet of all the horses I have known – and they have been many – I loved him the greatest. There was an indomitable fire in him that could never be extinguished.

Wondering what he had in store for me, I saddled and bridled Midnight while Bill put a halter on Moonlight, the mare. She was a silvery dapple grey, bedraggled now from the pouring rain.

As Bill led her close I swung up to Midnight. To ride a wild bucking horse on a bright sunny day is one thing. To ride Midnight, prince of all buck-jumpers, in a storming swish of rain is another – and how I did remains one of those things I often ponder over.

Twisting, swirling, sunfishing up to the topmost rails, and spinning down again, Midnight did his best. I did mine. We battled as we had many times before, and finally Midnight raised his head to walk quietly across to the mare.

When Bill handed me her lead rope, he said, "So help me, mate, how did you stay there? I shut my eyes when he went up on them rails."

I said, "It's gettin' so it's habit. Though one of these days I'll forget, an' he'll have me. So long, Bill, an' thanks for everything."

Bill called, "So long," and opened the gates to let me ride out.

Midnight strode forcibly, splattering mud in a long striding walk. Moonlight jogged by his side, serene, despite the torrential pourings which were beating over us.

For two or three hours the track we were following wound through flat, one-time dusty plains. Now they were great sheets of water, rippled and torn by the driving rain.

My concern as I rode, streaming wet in the saddle, was the river I would soon have to cross. If the bridge was still intact I would have little trouble. If it was damaged, only one course was left – swim the river, or turn back to Bill, who was running short of food. I felt that already I had imposed too much on his kindness. The gnawing thought was that he might be isolated and not get food for weeks if the rain kept on. And my being with him would aggravate, not help his situation.

When the timber-line of the river loomed through the scudding rain I had made up my mind – come what may, we had to cross. Midnight, I think, had done the same. He carried his ears pricked with eagerness, keen to get back to his home ground. But the possibilities looked grim as we neared the river's banks.

Normally sluggish, the river was tossing and boiling in flood. Instead of being thirty yards wide it was sixty or seventy, and still rising. Debris swirling in the current gave a good indication of this.

The bridge was awash, curled over with big cresting waves that looked frightening. And when I urged Midnight closer he snorted, warningly, stiffening the proud crest of his neck. Planting his fore-feet wide, he refused to be spurred on to the bridge's planking.

Knowing him, I said, "OK. We'll see what it's like up stream."

No horse understands words, of course, but they sense inflection. Midnight wheeled and, with Moonlight jogging beside him, headed up river. We reached a bend, then paused in shallow muddy water while I stared to mid-stream.

For a moment I wavered. The current swirled and slid in a forbidding manner. The eddies seemed to be ribbed one against the other. But Midnight shook his wet head impatiently, snatching at his bit for me to free him.

Thinking he might be of encouragement to Moonlight, I slipped her rope around Midnight's neck, then took two or three turns with the end. This allowed a fairly strong connection, yet one I could free quickly if needed.

And I remembered, numbed though I was in mind and body by the blinding pounding rain, noticing Moonlight's manner. She seemed oblivious of what storm, rain, and flood could so to her; as if greater things were encompassing her than the tortured swollen river.

She made no sound as Midnight nickered, striding strongly into the racing swirling flow. Soon he and Moonlight were shoulder deep, breasting into the deeper water. And suddenly I felt the pull as the current snatched at them both.

The snatch was so strong, and the smashing beat of rain so great, I had no sense of the horses swimming. Though their legs must have been driving with all the strength they possessed, I felt only the sucking boiling river pulling us on. It seemed I was smothering from water churned around from above and below.

Yet slowly but surely Midnight breasted his way against the torrent. Moonlight swam with him, keeping shoulder close to my knee, and sheltered to some extent by Midnight's powerful body.

When we were halfway between the bend and the bridge I judged we were heading fairly right; another thirty yards would diagonally bring us into shallow water, where the horses could fight for a footing.

But thirty yards in a roaring foaming river, ripped to frightening force by flood, seems unending. The blinding rain made judgement difficult, too, and

when I glanced around to see a huge snag bearing down on us I thought the end had come.

But there is always a will that fights against extremities. The will this time was Midnight. From depths of strength known only to his wild tough spirit he surged forward taking Moonlight with him.

The snag swirled past, barely missing their tails. If ever a man felt his love for an animal grow to a greatness beyond words, I did at that moment. It's a memory I treasure from there and for all time.

We were closer to the broken bridge than I had estimated when the horses floundered to their feet. Luckily the bank was silted over with sand and not mud, which might have been a death trap.

Riding out from the seething reddish water, I patted Midnight's neck, then Moonlight's. They both shook their streaming heads, eager to be on the move again, so we rode on in the rain.

If anything it increased in force until everything seemed a sodden blur which was washing right through me. Then I felt Moonlight begin to drag on her rope. As if ordered, Midnight came to a stop and stood with his head to the rain while I slid from the soggy saddle.

Bush horses are not nurtured products of stables and veterinary surgeons. Their lives follow a cycle where birth and death are natural. Moonlight lay down on the soaked streaming ground and, without undue stress or strain, gave birth to a colt who, at first, didn't like the world he was born into. But after a puzzled sniff or two he scrambled up with his mother, to stand shivering wetly by her side. She licked his ears then, despite the rain, licked some semblance of warmth into his tiny hopeful body. Midnight whinnied, excited – as geldings always are – to see a new foal wobbling near him.

Numbed more than ever, I had to decide what to do. Moonlight could travel on, but the colt couldn't. His little legs and hooves would take several hours to strengthen, and I still had about ten miles to go. Scuffing water from my face I decided to attempt the impossible – put the little chap up in front of my saddle and hope Midnight wouldn't throw the two of us.

As I have said, Midnight was a strange horse. A mixture of brumbie and outlaw blood made him dangerous, and no one else had ever ridden him except me. Yet he stood like a rock while I slid the colt on to his withers, then mounted.

For an awful chilled moment I thought he was going to buck – throw the colt and me if he could, into the rain-splashed puddles. Then he stepped out smartly, bearing us both without effort. Moonlight strode with him, pacing step for step. From there on the miles were a rain-drenched curtain through which we had to pass.

Reaching the homestead I shut Moonlight and her foal in a stall where straw was fetlock deep. Hay, too, hung from the pine wall racks.

Midnight I turned loose. He was that kind of horse – no softness; no gentleness; just sheer hard endurance, bred to all kinds of weather.

And as he splashed away, whinnying for his mates somewhere out in the darkness, I remembered the river. Only a horse of Midnight's calibre could have borne me across it. And only Midnight knew the closeness of Moonlight's need.

Is it any wonder that I loved him?

Jumble

Richmal Crompton

Willam's father carefully placed the bow and
arrow at the back of the library cupboard,
then closed the cupboard door and locked it in grim
silence. William's eyes, large, reproachful, and
gloomy, followed every movement.

"Three windows and Mrs Clive's cat all in one
morning," began Mr Brown sternly.

"I didn't *mean* to hit that cat," said William
earnestly. "I didn't – honest. I wouldn't go round
teasin' cats. They get so mad at you, cats do. It jus'
got in the way. I couldn't stop shootin' in time. An' I
didn't *mean* to break those windows. I wasn't *tryin'*
to hit them. I've not hit anything I was trying to hit
yet," wistfully. "I've not got into it. It's jus' a knack.
It jus' wants practice."

Mr Brown pocketed the key.

"'It's a knack you aren't likely to acquire by
practice on this instrument," he said drily.

William wandered out into the garden and looked sadly up at the garden wall. The Little Girl Next Door was away and could offer no sympathy, even if he climbed up to his precarious seat on the top. Fate was against him in every way. With a deep sigh he went out of the garden gate and strolled down the road disconsolately, hands in pockets.

Life stretched empty and uninviting before him without his bow and arrow. And Ginger would have his bow and arrow, Douglas would have his bow and arrow. He, William, alone would be a thing apart, a social outcast, a boy without a bow and arrow; for bows and arrows were the fashion. If only one of the others would break a window or hit a silly old cat that hadn't the sense to keep out of the way.

He came to a stile leading into a field and took his seat upon it dejectedly, his elbows on his knees, his chin in his hands. Life was simply not worth living.

"A rotten old cat!" he said aloud, "a rotten old cat – and didn't even hurt it. It – it made a fuss – jus' out of spite, screamin' and carryin' on! And windows! – as if glass wasn't cheap enough – and easy to put in. I could mend 'em myself – if I'd got the stuff to do it. I—" He stopped. Something was coming down the road. It came jauntily with a light, dancing step, fox-terrier ears cocked, retriever nose raised, collie tail wagging, slightly-dachshund body a-quiver with the joy of life.

It stopped in front of William with a glad bark of welcome, then stood eager, alert, friendly, a mongrel unashamed.

"Rats! Fetch 'em out!" said William idly.

It gave a little spring and waited, front paws apart and crouching, a waggish eye upraised to William. William broke off a stick from the hedge and threw it. His visitor darted after it with a shrill bark, took it up, worried it, threw it in the air, caught it, growled at it, finally brought it back to William and waited, panting, eager, unmistakably grinning, begging for more.

William's drooping spirits revived. He descended from his perch and examined its collar. It bore one word "Jumble".

"Hey! Jumble!" he called, setting off down the road.

Jumble jumped up around him, dashed off, dashed back, worried his boots, jumped up at him again in wild, eager friendship, dashed off again, begged for another stick, caught it, rolled over with it, growled at it, then chewed it up and laid the remains at William's feet.

"Good ole chap!" said William encouragingly. "Good ole Jumble! Come on, then."

Jumble came on. William walked through the village with a self-conscious air of proud yet careless ownership, while Jumble gambolled round his heels.

Every now and then he would turn his head and whistle imperiously, to recall his straying *protégé* from the investigation of ditches and roadside. It was a whistle, commanding, controlling, yet withal careless, that William had sometimes practised privately in readiness for the blissful day when Fate should present him with a real live dog of his own. So far Fate, in the persons of his father and mother, had been proof against all his pleadings.

William passed a blissful morning. Jumble swam in the pond, he fetched sticks out of it, he shook himself violently all over William, he ran after a hen, he was chased by a cat, he barked at a herd of cows, he pulled down a curtain that was hanging out in a cottage garden to dry – he was mischievous, affectionate, humorous, utterly irresistible – and he completely adopted William. William would turn a corner with a careless swagger and then watch breathlessly to see if the rollicking, frisky little figure would follow, and always it came tearing eagerly after him.

William was rather late to lunch. His father and mother and elder brother and sister were just beginning the meal. He slipped quietly and unostentatiously into his seat. His father was reading a newspaper. Mr Brown always took two daily papers, one of which he perused at breakfast and the other at lunch.

"William," said Mrs Brown, "I do wish you'd be in time, and I do wish you'd brush your hair before you come to table."

William raised a hand to perform the operation, but catching sight of its colour, hastily lowered it.

"No, Ethel dear, I didn't know anyone had taken Lavender Cottage. An artist? How nice! William dear, *do* sit still. Have they moved in yet?"

"Yes," said Ethel, "they've taken it furnished for two months, I think. Oh, my goodness, just *look* at William's hands!"

William put his hands under the table and glared at her.

"Go and wash your hands, dear," said Mrs Brown patiently.

For eleven years she had filled the trying position of William's mother. It had taught her patience.

William rose reluctantly.

"They're not dirty," he said in a tone of righteous indignation. "Well, anyway, they've been dirtier other times and you've said nothin'. I can't be *always* washin' them, can I? Some sorts of hands get dirty quicker than others an' if you keep on washing' it

102

only makes them worse an'—"

Ethel groaned and William's father lowered his paper. William withdrew quickly but with an air of dignity.

"And just *look* at his boots!" said Ethel as he went. "Simply caked; and his stockings are soaking wet – you can see from here. He's been right *in* the pond by the look of him and—"

William heard no more. There were moments when he actively disliked Ethel.

He returned a few minutes later, shining with cleanliness, his hair brushed back fiercely off his face.

"His *nails*," murmured Ethel as he sat down.

"Well," said Mrs Brown, "go on telling us about the new people. William, do hold your knife properly, dear. Yes, Ethel?"

William finished his meal in silence, then brought forth his momentous announcement.

"I've gotter dog," he said with an air of importance.

"What sort of a dog?" and "Who gave it to you?" said Robert and Ethel simultaneously.

"No one gave it me," he said. "I jus' got it. It began following me this morning an' I couldn't get rid of it. It wouldn't go, anyway. It followed me all round the village an' it came home with me. I couldn't get rid of it, anyhow."

"Where is it now?" said Mrs Brown anxiously.

"In the back garden."

Mr Brown folded up his paper.

"Digging up my flower-beds, I suppose," he said with despairing resignation.

"He's tied up all right," William reassured him. "I tied him to the tree in the middle of the rose-bed."

"The rose-bed!" groaned his father. "Good Lord!"

"Has he had anything to eat?" demanded Robert sternly.

"Yes," said William, avoiding his mother's eye. "I found a few bits of old things for him in the larder."

William's father took out his watch and rose from the table.

"Well, you'd better take it to the Police Station this afternoon," he said, shortly.

'The Police Station!" repeated William hoarsely. "It's not a *lost* dog. It – jus' doesn't belong to anyone, at least it didn't. Poor thing," feelingly. "It – it doesn't want *much* to make it happy. It can sleep in my room an' jus' eat scraps."

Mr Brown went out without answering.

"You'll have to take it, you know, William," said Mrs Brown, "so be quick. You know where the Police Station is, don't you? Shall I come with you?"

"No, thank you," said William hastily.

A few minutes later he was walking down to the

Police Station followed by the still eager Jumble, who trotted along, unconscious of his doom.

Upon William's face was a set, stern expression which cleared slightly as he neared the Police Station. He stood at the gate and looked at Jumble. Jumble placed his front paws ready for a game and wagged his tail.

"Well," said William, "here you are. Here's the Police Station."

Jumble gave a shrill bark. "Hurry up with that stick or that race, whichever you like," he seemed to say.

"Well, go in," said William, nodding his head in the direction of the door.

Jumble began to worry a big stone in the road. He rolled it along with his paws, then ran after it with fierce growls.

"Well, it's the Police Station," said William. "Go in if you want."

With that he turned on his heel and walked home, without one backward glance. But he walked slowly, with many encouraging "Hey! Jumbles" and many short commanding whistles. And Jumble trotted happily at his heels. There was no one in the garden, there was no one in the hall, there was no one on the stairs. Fate was for once on William's side.

William appeared at the tea-table well washed and

brushed, wearing that air of ostentatious virtue that those who knew him best connected with his most daring coups.

"Did you take that dog to the Police Station, William?" said William's father.

William coughed.

"Yes, Father," he said meekly with his eyes upon his plate.

"What did they say about it?"

"Nothing, Father."

"I suppose I'd better spend the evening replanting those rose-trees," went on his father bitterly.

"And William gave him a *whole* steak and kidney pie," murmured Mrs Brown. "Cook will have to make another for tomorrow."

William coughed again politely, but did not raise his eyes from his plate.

"What is that noise?" said Ethel. "Listen!"

They sat, listening intently. There was a dull grating sound as of the scratching of wood.

"It's upstairs," said Robert with the air of a Sherlock Holmes.

Then came a shrill, impatient bark.

"It's a *dog*!" said the four of them simultaneously. "It's William's dog."

They all turned horrified eyes upon William, who coloured slightly but continued to eat a piece of cake with an unconvincing air of abstraction.

"I thought you said you'd taken that dog to the Police Station, William," said Mr Brown sternly.

"I did," said William with decision. "I did take it to the Police Station an' I came home. I s'pose it must of got out an' come home an' gone into my bedroom."

"Where did you leave it? In the Police Station?"

"No – at it – jus' at the gate."

Mr Brown rose with an air of weariness.

"Robert," he said, "will you please see that that animal goes to the Police Station this evening?"

"Yes, Father," said Robert, with a vindictive glare at William.

William followed him upstairs.

"Beastly nuisance!" muttered Robert.

Jumble, who was chewing William's door, greeted them ecstatically.

"Look!" said William bitterly. "Look at how it knows one! Nice thing to send a dog that knows one like that to the Police Station! Mean sort of trick!"

Robert surveyed it coldly.

"Rotten little mongrel!" he said from the heights of superior knowledge.

"Mongrel!" said William indignantly. "There jus' isn't no mongrel about *him*. Look at him! An' he can learn tricks easy as easy. Look at him sit up and beg. I only taught him this afternoon."

He took a biscuit out of his pocket and held it up. Jumble rose unsteadily on to his hind legs and tumbled over backwards. He wagged his tail and grinned, intensely amused. Robert's expression of superiority relaxed.

"Do it again," he said. "Not so far back. Here! Give it me. Come on, come on, old chap! That's it! Now stay there! Stay there! Good dog! Got any more? Let's try him again."

During the next twenty minutes they taught him to sit up and almost taught him "Trust" and "Paid for". There was certainly a charm about Jumble. Even Robert felt it. Then Ethel's voice came up the stairs.

"Robert! Sydney Bellew's come for you."

"Blow the wretched dog!" said the fickle Robert rising, red and dishevelled from stooping over Jumble. "We were going to walk to Fairfields and the beastly Police Station's right out of our way."

"I'll take it, Robert," said William kindly. "I will really."

Robert eyed him suspiciously.

"Yes, you took it this afternoon, didn't you?"

"I will, honest, tonight, Robert. Well, I couldn't, could I? – after all this."

"I don't know," said Robert darkly. "No one ever knows what *you* are going to do!"

Sydney's voice came up.

"Hurry up, old chap! We shall never have time to do it before dark, if you aren't quick."

"I'll take him, honest, Robert."

Robert hesitated and was lost.

"Well," he said, "you just mind you do, that's all, or I'll jolly well hear about it. I'll see *you* do too."

So William started off once more towards the Police Station with Jumble, still blissfully happy, at his heels. William walked slowly, eyes fixed on the ground, brows knit in deep thought. It was very rarely that William admitted himself beaten.

"Hello, William!"

William looked up.

Ginger stood before him holding his bow and arrows ostentatiously.

"You've had your bow and arrow took off you!" he jeered.

William fixed his eye moodily upon him for a minute, then very gradually his eye brightened and his face cleared. William had an idea.

"If I give you a dog half time," he said slowly, "will you give me your bow and arrow half time?"

"Where's your dog?" said Ginger suspiciously.

William did not turn his head.

"There's one behind me, isn't there," he said anxiously. "Hey, Jumble!"

"Oh, yes, he's just come out of the ditch."

"Well," continued William, "I'm taking him to the Police Station and I'm just goin' on an' he's following me and if you take him off me I won't see you 'cause I won't turn round and jus' take hold of his collar an' he's called Jumble an' take him up to the old barn and we'll keep him there an' share him and feed him days and days about and you let me practise on your bow and arrow. That's fair, isn't it?"

Ginger considered thoughtfully.

"All right," he said laconically.

William walked on to the Police Station without turning round.

"Well?" whispered Robert sternly that evening.

"I took him, Robert – least – I started off with him, but when I'd got there he'd gone. I looked round and he'd jus' gone. I couldn't see him anywhere, so I came home."

"Well, if he comes to this house again," said Robert, "I'll wring his neck, so just you look out."

Two days later William sat in the barn on an upturned box, chin in hands, gazing down at Jumble. A paper bag containing Jumble's ration for the day lay beside him. It was his day of ownership. The collecting of Jumble's "scraps" was a matter of infinite care and trouble. They consisted of: a piece of bread that William had managed to slip into his pocket during breakfast, a piece of meat he had managed to slip into his pocket during dinner, a jam puff stolen from the larder and a bone removed from the dustbin. Ginger roamed the fields with his bow and arrow while William revelled in the ownership of Jumble. Tomorrow William would roam the fields with bow and arrow and Ginger would assume ownership of Jumble.

William had spent the morning teaching Jumble several complicated tricks, and adoring him more and more completely each moment. He grudged him bitterly to Ginger, but – the charm of the bow and arrow was strong. He wished to terminate the partnership, to resign Ginger's bow and arrow and take the irresistible Jumble wholly to himself. He thought of the bow and arrow in the library cupboard; he thought, planned, plotted, but could find no way out. He did not see a man come to the door of the barn and stand there leaning against the door-post watching him. He was a tall man with a thin, lean face and a loose-fitting tweed suit. As his eyes lit upon William and Jumble they narrowed suddenly and his mobile lips curved into a slight, unconscious smile. Jumble saw him first and went towards him wagging his tail. William looked up and scowled ungraciously. The stranger raised his hat.

"Good afternoon," he said politely. "Do you remember what you were thinking about just then?"

William looked at him with a certain interest, speculating upon his probable insanity. He imagined lunatics were amusing people.

"Yes."

"Well, if you'll think of it again and look just like that, I'll give you anything you like. It's a rash promise, but I will."

William promptly complied. He quite forgot the presence of the strange man, who took a little block out of his pocket and began to sketch William's inscrutable, brooding face.

"Daddy!"

The man sighed and put away his block.

"You'll do it again for me one day, won't you, and I'll keep my promise. Hello!"

A little girl appeared now at the barn door, dainty, dark-eyed and exquisitely dressed. She threw a lightning flash at the occupants of the barn.

"Daddy!" she screamed. "It's Jumble! It *is* Jumble! Oh, you horrid dog-stealing boy!"

Jumble ran to her with shrill barks of welcome, then ran back to William to reassure him of his undying loyalty.

"It *is* Jumble," said the man. "He's called Jumble," he explained to William, "because he is a jumble. He's all sorts of a dog, you know. This is Ninette, my daughter, and my name is Jarrow, and we've taken Lavender Cottage for two months. We're roving vagabonds. We never stay anywhere longer than two months. So now you know all about us. Jumble seems to have adopted you. Ninette, my dear, you are completely ousted from Jumble's heart. This gentleman reigns supreme."

"I *didn't* steal him," said William indignantly. "He just came. He began following me. I didn't want him to – not jus' at first anyway, not much anyway. I suppose," a dreadful fear came to his heart, "I suppose you want him back?"

"You can keep him for a bit if you want him, can't

he, Daddy? Daddy's going to buy me a Pom – a dear little white Pom. When we lost Jumble, I thought I'd rather have a Pom. Jumble's so rough and he's not really a *good* dog. I mean he's no pedigree."

"Then can I keep him jus' for a bit?" said William, his voice husky with eagerness.

"Oh, yes. I'd much rather have a quieter sort of dog. Would you like to come and see our cottage? It's just over here."

William, slightly bewildered, but greatly relieved, set off with her. Mr Jarrow followed slowly behind. It appeared that Miss Ninette Jarrow was rather a wonderful person. She was eleven years old. She had visited every capital in Europe, seen the best art and heard the best music in each. She had been to every play then on in London. She knew all the newest dances.

"Do you like Paris?" she asked William as they went towards Lavender Cottage.

"Never been there," said William stolidly, glancing round surreptitiously to see that Jumble was following.

She shook her dark curly head from side to side – a little trick she had.

"You funny boy. *Mais vous parlez francais, n'est ce pas?*"

William disdained to answer. He whistled to

114

Jumble, who was chasing an imaginary rabbit in a ditch.

"Can you jazz?" she asked.

"I don't know," he said guardedly. "I've not tried. I expect I could."

She took a few flying graceful steps with slim black silk-encased legs.

"That's it. I'll teach you at home. We'll dance it to a gramophone."

William walked on in silence.

She stopped suddenly under a tree and held up her little vivacious, piquant face to him.

"You can kiss me if you like," she said.

William looked at her dispassionately.

"I don't want to, thanks," he said politely.

"Oh, you *are* a funny boy!" she said with a ripple of laughter, "and you look so rough and untidy. You're rather like Jumble. Do you like Jumble?"

"Yes," said William. His voice had a sudden quaver in it. His ownership of Jumble was a thing of the past.

"You can have him for always and always," she said suddenly. "*Now* kiss me!"

He kissed her cheek awkwardly with the air of one determined to do his duty, but with a great, glad relief at his heart.

"I'd love to see you dance," she laughed. "You *would* look funny."

She took a few more fairy steps.

"You've seen Pavlova, haven't you?"

"Dunno."

"You must know."

"I mustn't," said William irritably. "I might have seen him and not known it was him, mightn't?"

She raced back to her father with another ripple of laughter. "He's *such* a funny boy, Daddy, and he can't jazz and he's never seen Pavlova, and he can't talk French and I've given him Jumble and he didn't want to kiss me!"

Mr Jarrow fixed William with a drily quizzical smile.

"Beware, young man," he said. "She'll try to educate you. I know her. I warn you."

As they got to the door of Lavender Cottage he turned to William.

"Now just sit and think for a minute. I'll keep my promise."

"I do like you," said Ninette graciously as he took his departure. "You must come again. I'll teach you heaps of things. I think I'd like to marry you when we grow up. You're so – *restful*."

William came home the next afternoon to find Mr Jarrow in the armchair in the library talking to his father.

"I was just dry for a subject," he was saying; "at my

wits' end, and when I saw them there, I had a Heaven-sent inspiration. Ah! here he is. Ninette wants you to come to tea tomorrow, William. Ninette's given him Jumble. Do you mind?" turning to Mr Brown.

Mr Brown swallowed hard.

"I'm trying not to," he said. "He kept us all awake last night, but I supposed we'll get used to it."

"And I made him a rash promise," went on Mr Jarrow, "and I'm jolly well going to keep it if it's humanly possible. William, what would you like best in all the world?"

William fixed his eyes unflinchingly upon his father.

"I'd like my bow and arrows back out of that cupboard," he said firmly.

Mr Jarrow looked at William's father beseechingly.

"Don't let me down," he implored. "I'll pay for all the damage."

Slowly and with a deep sigh Mr Brown drew a bunch of keys from his pocket.

"It means that we all go once more in hourly peril of our lives," he said resignedly.

After tea William set off again down the road. The setting sun had turned the sky to gold. There was a soft haze over all the countryside. The clear bird songs filled all the air, and the hedgerows were bursting into summer. And through it all marched William, with a slight swagger, his bow under one arm, his arrows under the other, while at his heels trotted Jumble, eager, playful, adoring – a mongrel unashamed – all sorts of a dog. And at William's heart was a proud, radiant happiness.

There was a picture in that year's Academy that attracted a good deal of attention. It was of a boy sitting on an upturned box in a barn, his elbows on his knees, his chin in his hands. He was gazing down at a mongrel dog and in his freckled face was the solemnity and unconscious, eager wistfulness that is the mark of youth. His untidy, unbrushed hair stood up round his face. The mongrel was looking up, expectant, trusting, adoring, some reflection of the boy's eager wistfulness showing in the eyes and cocked ears. It was called "Friendship".

Mrs Brown went up to see it. She said it wasn't really a very good likeness of William and she wished they'd made him look a little tidier.

The Happy Prince

Oscar Wilde

High above the city, on a tall column, stood the statue of the Happy Prince. He was gilded all over with thin leaves of fine gold, for eyes he had two bright sapphires, and a large red ruby glowed on his sword-hilt.

He was very much admired indeed. "He is as beautiful as a weathercock," remarked one of the Town Councillors who wished to gain a reputation for having artistic tastes; "only not quite so useful," he added, fearing lest people should think him unpractical, which he really was not.

"Why can't you be like the Happy Prince?" asked a sensible mother of her little boy who was crying for the moon. "The Happy Prince never dreams of crying for anything."

"I am glad there is someone in the world who is quite happy," muttered the disappointed man as he gazed at the wonderful statue.

"He looks just like an angel," said the Charity Children as they came out of the cathedral in their bright scarlet cloaks and their clean white pinafores.

"How do you know?" said the Mathematical Master, "you have never seen one."

"Ah! but we have, in our dreams," answered the children; and the Mathematical Master frowned and looked very severe, for he did not approve of children dreaming.

One night there flew over the city a little Swallow. His friends had gone away to Egypt six weeks before, but he had stayed behind, for he was in love with the most beautiful Reed. He had met her early in the spring as he was flying down the river after a big yellow moth, and had been so attracted by her slender waist that he had stopped to talk to her.

"Shall I love you?" said the Swallow, who liked to come to the point at once, and the Reed made him a low bow. So he flew round and round her, touching the water with his wings, and making silver ripples. This was his courtship, and it lasted all through the summer.

"It is a ridiculous attachment," twittered the other Swallows; "she has no money, and far too many relations"; and indeed the river was quite full of Reeds. Then, when the autumn came they all flew away.

After they had gone he felt lonely, and began to tire of his lady-love. "She has no conversation," he said, "and I am afraid that she is a coquette, for she is always flirting with the wind." And certainly, whenever the wind blew, the Reed made the most beautiful curtsies. "I admit that she is domestic," he continued, "but I love travelling and my wife, consequently, should love travelling also."

"Will you come away with me?" he said finally to her, but the Reed shook her head, she was so attached to her home.

"You have been trifling with me," he cried. "I am off to the Pyramids. Goodbye!" and he flew away.

All day long he flew, and at night-time he arrived at the city. "Where shall I put up?" he said, "I hope the town has made preparations."

Then he saw the statue on the tall column.

"I will put up there," he cried; "it is a fine position, with plenty of fresh air." So he alighted just between the feet of the Happy Prince.

"I have a golden bedroom," he said softly to himself as he looked around, and he prepared to go to sleep; but just as he was putting his head under his wing a large drop of water fell on him. "What a curious thing!" he cried "there is not a single cloud in the sky, the stars are quite clear and bright, and yet it is raining. The climate in the north of Europe

is really dreadful. The Reed used to like the rain, but that was merely her selfishness."

Then another drop fell.

"What is the use of a statue if it cannot keep the rain off?" he said; "I must look for a good chimney-pot," and he determined to fly away.

But before he had opened his wings, a third drop fell, and he looked up, and saw – Ah! what did he see?

The eyes of the Happy Prince were filled with tears, and tears were running down his golden cheeks. His face was so beautiful in the moonlight that the little Swallow was filled with pity.

"Who are you?" he said.

"I am the Happy Prince."

"Why are you weeping then?" asked the Swallow; "you have quite drenched me."

"When I was alive and had a human heart," answered the statue, "I did not know what tears were, for I lived in the Palace of Sans-Souci, where sorrow is not allowed to enter. In the daytime I played with my companions in the garden, and in the evening I led the dance in the Great Hall. Round the garden ran a very lofty wall, but I never cared to ask what lay beyond it, everything about me was so beautiful. My courtiers called me the Happy Prince, and happy indeed I was, if pleasure is happiness. So I lived, and so I died. And now that I am dead they have set me up here so high that I can see all the ugliness and all the misery of my city, and though my heart is made of lead yet I cannot choose but weep."

"What! Is he not solid gold?" said the Swallow to himself. He was too polite to make any personal remarks out loud.

"Far away," continued the statue in a low musical voice, "far away in a little street there is a poor house. One of the windows is open, and through it I can see a woman seated at a table. Her face is thin and worn, and she has coarse, red hands, all pricked by the needle, for she is a seamstress. She is embroidering passion-flowers on a satin gown for the loveliest of the Queen's maids-of-honour to wear at the next Court ball. In a bed in the corner of the room her little boy is lying ill. He has a fever, and is asking for oranges. His mother has nothing to give him but river water, so he is crying. Swallow, Swallow, little Swallow, will you not bring her the ruby out of my sword-hilt? My feet are fastened to this pedestal and I cannot move."

"I am waited for in Egypt," said the Swallow. "My friends are flying up and down the Nile, and talking to the large lotus-flowers. Soon they will go to sleep in the tomb of the great King. The King is there himself in his painted coffin. He is wrapped in yellow linen, and embalmed with spices. Round his neck is a chain of pale green jade, and his hands are like withered leaves."

"Swallow, Swallow, little Swallow," said the Prince, "will you not stay with me for one night, and be my messenger? The boy is so thirsty, and the mother so sad."

"I don't think I like boys," answered the Swallow. "Last summer, when I was staying on the river, there were two rude boys, the miller's sons, who were always throwing stones at me. They never hit me, of course; we swallows fly far too well for that, and besides I come of a family famous for its agility; but still, it was a mark of disrespect."

But the Happy Prince looked so sad that the little Swallow was sorry. "It is very cold here," he said; "but I will stay with you for one night, and be your messenger."

"Thank you, little Swallow," said the Prince.

So the Swallow picked out the great ruby from the Prince's sword, and flew away with it in his beak over the roofs of the town.

He passed by the cathedral tower, where the white marble angels were sculptured. He passed by the palace and heard the sound of dancing. A beautiful girl came out on the balcony with her lover. "How wonderful the stars are," he said to her, "and how wonderful is the power of love!"

"I hope my dress will be ready in time for the State ball," she answered; "I have ordered passion-flowers to be embroidered on it: but the seamstresses are so lazy."

He passed over the river, and saw the lanterns hanging to the masts of the ships. He passed over the Ghetto, and saw the old Jews bargaining with each other, and weighing out money in copper scales. At last he came to the poor house and looked in. The boy was tossing feverishly on his bed, and the mother had fallen asleep, she was so tired. In he hopped, and laid the great ruby on the table beside the woman's thimble. Then he flew gently round the bed, fanning the boy's forehead with his wings. "How cool I feel!" said the boy, "I must be getting better"; and he sank into a delicious slumber.

Then the Swallow flew back to the Happy Prince, and told him what he had done. "It is curious," he remarked, "but I feel quite warm now, although it is so cold."

"That is because you have done a good action," said the Prince. And the little Swallow began to think, and then he fell asleep. Thinking always made him sleepy.

When day broke he flew down to the river and had a bath. "What a remarkable phenomenon!" said the Professor of Orthithology as he was passing over the bridge. "A swallow in winter!" And he wrote a long letter about it to the local newspaper. Everyone quoted it, it was full of so many words that they could not understand.

"Tonight I go to Egypt," said the Swallow, and he was in high spirits at the prospect. He visited all the public monuments, and sat for a long time on top of the church steeple. Wherever he went the Sparrows chirruped, and said to each other, "What a distinguished stranger!" so he enjoyed himself very much.

When the moon rose he flew back to the Happy Prince. "Have you any commissions for Egypt?" he cried. "I am just starting."

"Swallow, Swallow, little Swallow," said the Prince, "will you not stay with me one night longer?"

"I am waited for in Egypt," answered the Swallow. "Tomorrow my friends will fly up to the Second Cataract. The river-horse couches there among the bulrushes, and on a great granite throne sits the God Memnon. All night long he watches the stars, and when the morning star shines he utters one cry of joy, and then he is silent. At noon the yellow lions come down to the water's edge to drink. They have eyes like green bells, and their roar is louder than the roar of the cataract."

"Swallow, Swallow, little Swallow," said the

Prince, "far away across the city I see a young man in a garret. He is leaning over a desk covered with papers, and in a tumbler by his side there is a bunch of withered violets. His hair is brown and crisp, and his lips are red as a pomegranate, and he has large and dreamy eyes. He is trying to finish a play for the Director of the Theatre, but he is too cold to write any more. There is no fire in the grate, and hunger has made him faint."

"I will wait with you one night longer," said the Swallow, who really had a good heart. "Shall I take him another ruby?"

"Alas! I have no ruby now," said the Prince, "my eyes are all that I have left. They are made of rare sapphires, which were brought out of India a thousand years ago. Pluck out one of them and take it to him. He will sell it to the jeweller, and buy firewood, and finish his play."

"Dear Prince," said the Swallow, "I cannot do that," and he began to weep.

"Swallow, Swallow, little Swallow," said the Prince, "do as I command you."

So the Swallow plucked out the Prince's eye, and flew away to the student's garret. It was easy enough to get in, as there was a hole in the roof. Through this he darted, and came into the room. The young man had his head buried in his hands, so he did not hear the flutter of the bird's wings, and when he looked up he found the beautiful sapphire lying on the withered violets.

"I am beginning to be appreciated," he cried; "this is from some great admirer. Now I can finish my play," and he looked quite happy.

The next day the Swallow flew down to the harbour. He sat on the mast of a large vessel and watched the sailors hauling big chests out of the hold with ropes. "Heave a-hoy!" they shouted as each chest came up. "I am going to Egypt!" cried the Swallow, but nobody minded, and when the moon rose he flew back to the Happy Prince.

"I am come to bid you goodbye," he cried.

"Swallow, Swallow, little Swallow," said the Prince, "will you not stay with me one night longer?"

"It is winter," answered the Swallow, "and the chill snow will soon be here. In Egypt the sun is warm on the green palm-trees, and the crocodiles lie in the mud and look lazily about them. My companions are building a nest in the Temple of Baalbek, and the pink and white doves are watching them, and cooing to each other. Dear Prince, I must leave you, but I will never forget you, and next spring I will bring you back two beautiful jewels in place of those you have given away. The ruby shall be redder than a red rose, and the sapphire shall be as blue as the great sea."

"In the square below," said the Happy Prince, "there stands a little match-girl. She has let her matches fall in the gutter, and they are all spoiled. Her father will beat her if she does not bring home some money, and she is crying. She has no shoes or stockings, and her little head is bare. Pluck out my other eye, and give it to her, and her father will not beat her."

"I will stay with you one night longer," said the Swallow, "but I cannot pluck out your eye. You would be quite blind then."

"Swallow, Swallow, little Swallow," said the Prince, "do as I command you."

So he plucked out the Prince's other eye, and darted down with it. He swooped past the match-girl, and slipped the jewel into the palm of her hand. "What a lovely bit of glass!" cried the little girl; and she ran home, laughing.

Then the Swallow came back to the Prince. "You are blind now," he said, "so I will stay with you always."

"No, little Swallow," said the poor Prince, "you must go away to Egypt."

"I will stay with you always," said the Swallow, and he slept at the Prince's feet.

All the next day he sat on the Prince's shoulder, and told him stories of what he had seen in strange lands. He told him of the red ibises, who stand in long rows on the banks of the Nile, and catch goldfish in their beaks; of the Sphinx, who is as old as the world itself, and lives in the desert, and knows everything; of the merchants, who walk slowly by the side of their camels and carry amber beads in their hands; of the King of the Mountains of the Moon, who is as black as ebony, and worships a large crystal; of the great green snake that sleeps in a palm-tree, and has twenty priests to feed it with honey-cakes; and of the pygmies who sail over a big lake on large flat leaves, and are always at war with the butterflies.

"Dear little Swallow," said the Prince, "you tell me

of marvellous things, but more marvellous than anything is the suffering of men and of women. There is no Mystery so great as Misery. Fly over my city, little Swallow, and tell me what you see there."

So the Swallow flew over the great city, and saw the rich making merry in the beautiful houses, while the beggars were sitting at the gates. He flew into dark lanes, and saw the white faces of starving children looking out listlessly at the black streets. Under the archway of a bridge two little boys were lying in one another's arms to try and keep themselves warm. "How hungry we are!" they said. "You must not lie here," shouted the watch-man, and they wandered out into the rain.

Then he flew back and told the Prince what he had seen.

"I am covered with fine gold," said the Prince, "you must take it off, leaf by leaf, and give it to my poor; the living always think that gold can make them happy."

Leaf after leaf of the fine gold the Swallow picked off, till the Happy Prince looked quite dull and grey. Leaf after leaf of the fine gold he brought to the poor, and the children's faces grew rosier, and they laughed and played games in the street. "We have bread now!" they cried.

Then the snow came, and after the snow came the

frost. The streets looked as if they were made of silver, they were so bright and glistening; long icicles like crystal daggers hung down from the eaves of the houses, everybody went about in furs, and the little boys wore scarlet caps and skated on the ice.

The poor little Swallow grew colder and colder, but he would not leave the Prince, he loved him too well. He picked up crumbs outside the baker's door when the baker was not looking, and tried to keep himself warm by flapping his wings.

But at last he knew that he was going to die. He had just enough strength to fly up to the Prince's shoulder once more. "Goodbye, dear Prince!" he murmured, "will you let me kiss your hand?"

"I am glad that you are going to Egypt at last, little Swallow," said the Prince, "you have stayed too long here but you must kiss me on the lips, for I love you."

"It is not to Egypt that I am going," said the Swallow. "I am going to the House of Death. Death is the brother of Sleep, is he not?"

And he kissed the Happy Prince on the lips, and feel down dead at his feet.

At that moment a curious crack sounded inside the statue, as if something had broken. The fact is that the leaden heart had snapped right in two. It certainly was a dreadfully hard frost.

Early the next morning the Mayor was walking in the square below in company with the Town Councillors. As they passed the column he looked up at the statue. "Dear me! how shabby the Happy Prince looks!" he said.

"How shabby, indeed," cried the Town Councillors, who always agreed with the Mayor; and they went up to look at it.

"The ruby has fallen out of his sword, his eyes are gone, and he is golden no longer," said the Mayor; "in fact, he is little better than a beggar!"

"Little better than a beggar," said the Town Councillors.

"And here is actually a dead bird at his feet!" continued the Mayor. "We must really issue a proclamation that birds are not to be allowed to die here." And the Town Clerk made a note of the suggestion.

So they pulled down the statue of the Happy Prince. "As he is no longer beautiful he is no longer useful," said the Art Professor at the University.

Then they melted the statue in a furnace, and the Mayor held a meeting of the Corporation to decide what was to be done with the metal. "We must have another statue, of course," he said, "and it shall be a statue of myself."

"Of myself," said each of the Town Councillors,

and they quarrelled. When I last heard of them they were quarrelling still.

"What a strange thing!" said the overseer of the workmen at the foundry. "This broken lead heart will not melt in the furnace. We must throw it away." So they threw it on a dust-heap where the dead Swallow was also lying.

"Bring me the two most precious things in the city," said God to one of His Angels; and the Angel brought Him the leaden heart and the dead bird.

"You have rightly chosen," said God, "for in my garden of Paradise this little bird shall sing for evermore, and in my city of gold the Happy Prince shall praise me."

The Boy and Nyange the Cow

Retold by Anne Gatti

There was once a boy who spent his days out on the plains looking after his father's cattle. He was a very good herdsman and his animals obeyed and trusted him.

When he arrived home at the end of a tiring day out in the hot sun his father, who was a mean, bad-tempered man, always had more work for him to do around the house. The boy's mother had died when he was a baby and his father left all the household chores to him. Because of this, the boy could never visit his friends or go to the dances that were held in nearby villages. The other boys and girls of his tribe, the Kikuyu, were sorry for him. Many of the girls thought he was very handsome and would have liked to get to know him.

But the boy was either far away, grazing his cattle,

or stuck indoors, mending or making things.

The boy did have one friend, though – a cow called Nyange. Nyange had a dark, glossy coat and magnificent white horns. She seemed to understand that he was lonely and grazed close by him to keep him company. Whenever he wandered away from her, she would moo and moo until he came back. The boy fed her titbits whenever he could get them and when he went to the clay mines he always brought her back chunks of the salty clay as a special treat.

The boy often talked to Nyange as if she were human. He didn't really expect her to understand but it was good to be able to tell her his feelings. One day, forgetting that she was only a cow, he said, "Move over a bit, Nyange, you're blocking my view of the cows over by the bushes."

Nyange took a few steps to the left, and went on grazing. The boy was amazed. Perhaps she just moved to get more grass, he thought. I'll say something else and see what happens.

"Nyange, go over there to the bushes and tell those cows to come back here. It's time to go home," he said.

Nyange lifted her head and looked at him as if to say, "If that's what you want." Then she ambled over to the other cows, mooed at them, and led them back to the boy.

He couldn't believe it: a cow that understood human language, and it was his. He threw his arms round Nyange and shouted with happiness. It didn't matter that his legs felt tired or that the flies had been biting him. He now had a very special friend and he could keep it a secret from his father.

When he got home he watered the cattle and put them into the kraal. Then he went indoors as if nothing had happened. As usual, his father was just on his way out to an evening of beer-drinking and left him lots of chores to do. But that night the boy didn't mind so much – he was so excited about his extraordinary cow.

Next morning, when he went to let out the cattle, he could hear Nyange mooing louder than all the others and she didn't stop until he went over to her and scratched behind her ears. She licked his hands and swished her tail as he led her out. He set off for the plains, with his friend swinging her great big shoulders beside him.

The years went by and the boy grew very tall and strong. Nyange still helped him to herd the other cattle, and he still talked to her and brought her salty clay whenever he could. But the boy was fed up. His father was away from home most of the time, going from village to village drinking beer, and the boy was lonely. He could hear the sound of loud singing and feet stamping and the beating of drums echoing across the plains and he longed to be dancing with all the other young people.

One day he had an idea. He would ask Nyange to look after the cattle while he went to a dance at a village close by.

Nyange swished her tail in agreement. The boy ran most of the way, and found that the dancers were delighted to see him. He talked and he danced. He told them that a friend of his was looking after his cattle. From time to time, though, he thought about the cattle and wondered if they were safe. He'd heard that cattle thieves from a nearby camp of Masai warriors had been raiding some of his neighbours' herds.

As the sun was setting the boy headed back towards his cattle. As soon as he spotted them safely grazing, with Nyange keeping a watchful eye on them, he sang out,

> "Nyange! Nyange!
> Round them up, bring them up, Nyange.
> Night has come, Nyange,
> Let's go home, Nyange."

Nyange swished her tail and rounded up the cattle, herding them towards the boy.

The boy was happier than he'd ever been. The

cattle were safe, he'd had a wonderful time, and now he could be like the other boys and girls and go to dances regularly.

He did go to dances regularly, and he became a very good dancer. On days when there were no dances, he would visit the new friends he had made and as the months went by he began to spend more and more time with one particular girl who had beautiful eyes and wore rows and rows of brightly coloured beads. But at sunset he always returned to his cattle and greeted Nyange with his song before leading them home. He told nobody about his special friend.

One day he went to a dance in a village several miles away and stayed there all day. It was almost dark by the time he arrived back at the spot where he had left Nyange and the herd. He sang his usual song, but nothing happened. No mooing from Nyange, no clang of cowbells, no clump of hooves moving towards him.

Maybe they've wandered over the hill, he thought. And he ran as fast as he could to the hilltop and sang again. Still nothing happened. He was now very worried. What if some Masai raiders had stolen Nyange and his herd? Everyone had been at the dance and they wouldn't have heard the cattle bellowing from that distance. What would his father say? How would they survive? How would he ever be able to pay for a wife?

He stumbled back through the dusky scrub to where he had last seen the cattle. He looked on the ground for clues about what might have happened. He noticed long footprints next to a flurry of hoof-marks and then he saw something red caught on a branch of a shrub. It was a piece of red cloth that looked as if it had been torn off a cloak.

"Masai!" he whispered into the night. He knew that the Masai liked to wear red clothes and paint their hair red.

The boy suddenly felt afraid. What should he do? If he followed the hoof-marks and caught up with the fierce Masai warriors they would probably kill him with their long spears. If he didn't try to get back the cattle, his father would certainly give him a terrible beating. And then he remembered Nyange. Poor Nyange, he thought. A prisoner in a strange country. Perhaps they won't even give her enough to eat and drink.

That decided him. Even if he could only save Nyange, it would be worth trying. Although it would have been wise to go home and fetch a war spear and shield, he decided not to waste any more time and he set off in the dark, armed only with the short spear and dagger that he normally carried in case lions or

141

hyenas attacked his herd.

All night long he followed the tracks – through bushes that scratched him, up steep mountains, across rivers. Sometimes he stopped to catch his breath, but after a minute or so he imagined he heard Nyange's deep mooing and set off again, determined to rescue her.

At dawn he climbed yet another mountain and by the time he had reached the top, which was surprisingly flat, the sun was beating down and he was longing for a drink. He looked down and saw a grassy valley below him. Dotted all along it, like muddy pools in a swamp, were herds of cattle grazing. There must have been hundreds of them, some brown, some white, some big and strong, others skinny and scrawny. In the middle, where smoke was drifting up from several fires, the boy could make out a Masai camp.

He sat down and stared at the scene below him. Tall men, with long plaited hair that glinted red in the bright light, moved among the cattle. Now and then he could see them poking the animals with the butt end of their long spears to keep them from straying. He shaded his eyes to see if he could pick out his herd. Suddenly he spotted Nyange's white horns. From where he was sitting, the herd she was with looked about the same size as his own. They

were close to the base of the mountain but there
would be no point, the boy told himself, in going
down to rescue them in broad daylight. He would
have to wait until nightfall.

Patiently, the boy watched the Masai camp all day
as he tried to work out a plan to steal back his herd.
He didn't stir, even to get a drink. As the distant
hilltops turned a beautiful reddish gold the Masai
started to gather round their fires to eat their
evening meal, leaving only a few warriors to guard
the herds. Soon the boy heard their songs and smelt
tantalizing wafts of roasted meat. The words of their
songs drifted up the mountain in the still night. The
Kikuyu people were useless, chanted the warriors.

They let the women cook their meals, they didn't know the first thing about cattle or how to look after them. The Kikuyu didn't deserve to own cattle. The Masai had a right to take the cattle from those useless Kikuyu.

The boy was furious to hear his people being insulted like this but the loud chantings of the warriors had given him an idea. He waited a few more hours till the valley grew silent except for the occasional clanking of a cow bell. The Masai were sleeping. He climbed down the mountain towards the valley as quietly as he could and stood on a rock near the bottom. Softly he sang.

> *"Nyange! Nyange!*
> *Round them up, bring them up, Nyange.*
> *Night has come, Nyange,*
> *Let's go home, Nyange."*

Straight away he heard a cow mooing. Could it be Nyange? Had she heard and understood him? He sang his greeting song again. This time he was sure the answering mooing was Nyange's and he stood there, his heart beating very fast as he listened to the sound of hooves cutting through the grass. They were moving in his direction and there seemed to be lots of them – many more than he was expecting.

He didn't have to wait long before he saw Nyange's

magnificent white horns approaching. He jumped off his rock and ran to greet her.

"Nyange! Nyange!" he whispered, "you are so clever. Are you all right? Can you make the journey back home?"

Nyange put her head down for the boy to scratch behind her ears and then licked his hand. The boy understood. She was saying "yes" to both his questions. He quickly explained to her the route he was going to take, and asked her to lead the rest of the huge herd that was appearing in front of him. He knew they would follow her.

He set off up the mountain and halfway up he cut around the side so that the cattle wouldn't be worn out too quickly from the steep climb. To his surprise the cattle didn't bellow or call as they normally did when travelling. Clever Nyange must have warned them to be silent.

It was only when the boy started to head round the side of the mountain that the Masai who were supposed to be on guard realized that all the cattle that were closest to the base of the mountain had gone. They roared and shouted, waking all the others, and frantically looked around to see where they had vanished. Then one of the guards spotted a light-coloured cow at the back of the herd scrambling up the mountainside. Several of the warriors ran after it, shouting and shaking their spears. They ran like the wind and soon caught up with the last of the escaping herd. But the cows at the back kicked out and bellowed as if they had gone mad and several of the Masai were knocked down and injured. Then, still bellowing like raging bulls, they charged away after the rest.

When the guards saw how fierce the cattle were, they went back down to the valley to ask their elders what to do. The elders listened to their story and said that the cattle must belong to the great god E-Ngai, and that he must have called the animals back to his kingdom in the sky. He was angry with the Masai, explained the elders, and would kill any warriors who followed the cattle up the mountain. As the first rays of the morning sun lit up the mountaintop, the elders fell to their knees and begged E-Ngai to forgive them for stealing his cattle.

So the Masai thieves did not follow the cattle and after a few hours, when the boy realized that for some reason he was not being chased, he stopped on the bank of a river. He bent down and took a long drink and so did the cattle. Now, for the first time, he could see how many cattle he was herding – there were at least three hundred of them, maybe more, flicking their tails and grazing peacefully at the water's edge.

After an hour's rest, the boy forded the river with

Nyange right behind him and the long train of cattle behind her, all obediently sploshing through the water and on towards the boy's home plains. He looked back and felt proud and excited: this was the greatest herd he had ever seen, and they were all obeying him. He led them at a steady pace, stopping every couple of hours to let them eat and drink.

It was midday on the following day when he climbed the hill overlooking his village. As he crossed the stretch of scrub that led to his home, a cloud of dust, which grew longer and longer as more cattle trod on the dry soil, hid most of the herd from view. The villagers, who had heard the rumble of their approaching footsteps, stood and gaped. As the boy drew closer, they could see more and more cattle emerging from the cloud as if by magic. The boy's father heard the commotion and joined his neighbours. He watched his son confidently leading this great army of cattle. For once he was speechless. He strode out to welcome his son home and as he did so the women of the village sang out their traditional welcome.

"Aaari-ririririri-ri!"

Father and son greeted each other and the rest of the villagers gathered round to hear the boy's story. The boy was thrilled to see that the girl with the beautiful eyes was standing at the front and smiling.

He told his tale about the Masai raid and how Nyange had saved his cattle and had made his father a rich man by adding so many cattle to the herd.

When the boy had finished, the father, who was bursting with pride in his brave and clever son, announced that he was throwing a feast for all the villagers in celebration of the boy's return. He then turned to the boy and said,

"Son, you may now have the wife of your own choice. I will offer however many cattle are required."

"Father, I have already chosen my bride, if she will have me," answered the boy and walked over to the girl with the beautiful eyes.

She smiled and thanked him, and said yes, she would very much like to marry him. Then she walked over to Nyange, who was standing patiently at the head of the herd, took off one of her bead necklaces and draped it across Nyange's forehead, from ear to ear.

"Thank you," she whispered, "for safely bringing back my husband-to-be."

Ike

Gary Paulsen

Much of my childhood I was alone. Family troubles – my parents were drunks – combined with a devastating shyness and a complete lack of social skills to ensure a life of solitude. This isolation was not natural, of course, especially for a child, and most of the time I was excruciatingly lonely. I sought friends whenever I could, but was rarely successful.

When I was very young these times of aloneness were spent making model airplanes, reading comic books or just daydreaming. But when I was twelve, living in a small town named Twin Forks in northern Minnesota, an uncle gave me a Remington .22 rifle he'd bought at a hardware store for ten dollars. I ran to the woods.

It is not somehow "politically correct" to hunt, and that is a shame for young boys. For me it was not only the opening into a world of wonder, it was salvation. I lived and breathed to hunt, to fish.

Two rivers ran out of town, one to the north and one to the east, and any day, hour or few minutes I could spare I would run these rivers. The first year I hunted mostly rabbits and ruffed grouse – feeding myself in the process. I scuffled along in old boots with a box of .22 long rifle cartridges in my pocket and the single-shot rifle in my hand. On my back was an old army surplus light pack I'd bought with money from setting pins at the local bowling alley. In the pack I had matches, usually a loaf of bread, salt and an old aluminium pot for boiling water.

There was great beauty in running the rivers, especially in the fall when the leaves were turning. The maples were red gold and filtered the sunlight so that you could almost taste the richness of the light, and before long I added a surplus army blanket, rolled up over the pack, and I would spend the nights out as well. During school – where I did badly – I would hunt in the evenings. But on Friday I was gone, and I would frequently spend the entire weekend alone in the woods.

The problem was that I was alone. I had not learned then to love solitude – as I do now – and the feeling of loneliness was visceral, palpable. I would see something beautiful – the sun through the leaves, a deer moving through the dappled light, the

explosion of a grouse flying up through the leaves –
and I would turn to point it out to somebody, turn to
say, "Look . . ." and there would be no one there.

The second fall after I'd started living in and off
the woods I decided to hunt ducks. Miles to the north
were the great swamps and breeding grounds of
literally millions of ducks and geese, and when the
migratory flights started south the sky would seem to
darken with them. The .22 rifle was not suited for
ducks – was indeed illegal for them – so I saved my
money setting pins and bought an old single-shot
Browning twelve-gauge shotgun from a kid named
Sonny. The gun had a long barrel and a full choke,
and with number four shot seemed to reach out
forever. I never became really good with it, but could
hit now and then when the ducks were flying at the
right angle. Duck hunting soon became my life.

I did not have decoys but I made some blinds six
miles out of town where there were cattail swamps. I
would walk out there in the dark, leaving the house
at three in the morning, nestle into the blinds and
wait for the morning flights to come in from the
north. Usually I would get one or two ducks – once a
goose – but some I wounded or didn't kill cleanly and
they would get into the swamp grass and weeds in the
water and I couldn't find them.

It was about then that I met Ike.

Ike was a great barrel-chested black Labrador that became one of the best friends I've ever had and was in all ways an equal; not a pet, not something to master, but an equal.

I had had other dogs. Snowball in the Philippines, then a cocker spaniel somebody gave me named Trina. They were sweet and dear and gave love the only way dogs can, with total acceptance, but Ike was the first dog I'd ever known not as a pet but as a separate entity, a partner.

We met strangely enough. It was duck season and I was going hunting. I woke up at three and sneaked from the basement, where I stayed when my parents were drunk – which was all the time – up into the kitchen. Quietly I made two fried egg sandwiches at the stove. I wrapped them in cellophane (this was well before sandwich bags), folded them into a paper sack and put them in my pack along with a Thermos of hot coffee. Then I got my shotgun from the basement. I dumped a box of shells into the pockets of the old canvas coat I'd found in a trunk in the back of the coal room. I put on the knee-high rubber boots I'd bought at army surplus.

I walked from the apartment building four blocks to the railroad, crossed the tracks near the round-house yard, crossed the Eighth Street bridge and then dropped down to the riverbank and started walking along the water.

The river quickly left settled country and headed into woods, and in the dark – there was just the faintest touch of grey on the horizon – it was hard going. The brush pulled at my clothes and after a mile and a half the swamps became more prevalent so that I was wading in muck. I went to pull myself up the bank and walk where the ground was harder.

It had been raining, mixed with snow, and the mud on the bank was as slick as grease. I fell once in the darkness, got to my feet and scrabbled up the bank again, shotgun in one hand and grabbing at roots and shrubs with the other. I had just gained the top, brought my head up over the edge, when a part of the darkness detached itself, leaned close to my face and went:

"Woof."

It was that distinct – not "arf", not "ruff", nor a growl, but the very defined sound of "woof".

I was so startled that I froze, mouth half open. Then I let go of the shrub and fell back down the mud incline. On the way down the thought hit me – bear. Something big and black, that sound – it had to be a bear. Then the word *gun*. I had a gun. I landed on my back and aimed up the bank, pulled the hammer back and put my finger on the trigger before I realized the gun wasn't loaded yet. I never loaded it while walking in the dark. I clawed at my pockets for shells, found one, broke open the gun and inserted the shell, slammed it shut and was going to aim again when something about the shape stopped me. (It was as well it did – I had accidentally jammed the barrel of the shotgun full of mud when I fell. Had I pulled the trigger the shell would have blown up in my face.)

There was just enough of dawn to show a silhouette. Whatever it was remained at the top of the bank. It was sitting there looking down at me and was the wrong shape and size for a bear. It was a big dog, a black dog. But it was a dog and it wasn't attacking.

I lowered the gun and wiped the mud out of my eyes, stood and scraped mud off my clothes. I was furious, but not at the dog. There were other hunters who worked the river during duck season and some of them had dogs. I assumed that one of them was nearby and had let his animal run loose, scaring about ten years off my life.

"Who owns you?" I asked the shape. It didn't move or make any further sounds and I climbed the bank again and it moved back a few feet, then sat again.

"Hello!" I called into the woods around me. "I have your dog here!"

There was nobody.

154

"So you're a stray?" There were many stray dogs in town and some of them ran to the woods. It was bad when they did because they often formed packs and did terrible damage. In packs they were worse than wolves because they did not fear man the way wolves did and they tore livestock and some people to pieces.

But strays were shy and usually starved. This dog stayed near me and in the gathering light I could see that he was a Labrador and that he was well fed. His coat was thick and he had fat on his back and sides.

"Well," I said. "What do I do with you?"

This time his tail thumped twice and he pointedly looked at the gun, then back at my face, then down the side of the river to the water.

"You want to hunt?"

There, he knew that word. His tail hammered his sides and he stood, wiggling, and moved off along the river ahead of me.

I had never hunted with a dog before and did not know for certain what was expected of me. But I started to follow, thinking we might jump up a mallard or teal. Then I remembered my fall and the mud and that the gun was still loaded. I unloaded it and checked the bore and found the end packed with mud. It took me a minute to clean it out and reload it and before I'd finished he'd come back and sat four feet away, watching me quietly.

It was light enough now for me to see that he had a collar and a tag so he wasn't a stray. It must be some town dog, I thought, that had followed me. I held out my hand. "Come here . . ."

But he remained at a distance and when it was obvious that I was ready to go he set off again. It was light enough now to shoot – light enough to see the front bead of the shotgun and a duck against the sky – so I kept the gun ready and we had not gone fifty yards when two mallards exploded out of some thick grass near the bank about twenty yards away and started up and across the river.

It was a classic shot. Mallards flying straight up to gain altitude before making off, backlit against a cold, cloudy October sky. I raised the gun, cocked it, aimed just above the right-hand duck to lead his flight and squeezed the trigger.

There was a crash and the recoil slammed me back. I was small and the gun was big and I usually had a bruise after firing it more than once. But my aim was good and the right-hand duck seemed to break in the air, crumpled and fell into the water. I had shot ducks over the river before and the way to get them was to wait until the current brought the body to shore. Sometimes it took most of the morning, waiting for the slow-moving water to bring them in.

This time was different. With the smell of powder still in the air, almost before the duck finished falling, the dog was off the bank in a great leap, hit the water swimming, his shoulders pumping as he churned the surface and made a straight line to the dead duck. He took it in his mouth gently, turned and swam back, climbed the bank and put the duck by my right foot, then moved off a couple of feet and sat, looking at me.

I made sure the duck was dead, then picked it up and tied it to my belt with a string I carried for the purpose. The dog sat and watched me the whole time, waiting. It was fully light now and I moved to him,

petted him – he let me but in a reserved way – and pulled his tag to the side so I could read it.

My name is Ike.

That's all it said. No address, no owner's name, just one short sentence.

"Well, Ike" – at this his tail wagged – "I'd like to thank you for bringing me the duck . . ."

And that was how it started, how I came to know Ike.

Duck season soon consumed me and I spent every morning walking and hunting the river. On school days I would go out and come back just in time to get to classes and on the weekends I stayed out.

And every morning Ike was there. I'd come across the bridge, start down the river, and he'd be there, waiting. After a few mornings he'd let me pet him – I think he did it for me more than him – and by the end of the first week I was looking forward to seeing him. By the middle of the second week I felt as if we'd been hunting with each other forever.

And he knew hunting. Clearly somebody had trained him well. He moved quietly, sat in the blind with me without moving, watched the barrel of the gun to see which duck I was going to shoot at, and when I shot he would leap into the water. On those occasions when I missed – I think more often than not – he would watch the duck fly away, turn to me and give me a look of such uncompromising pity and scorn that I would feel compelled to apologize and make excuses.

"The wind moved the barrel," or "A drop of water hit my eye when I shot."

Of course, he did not believe me but would turn back, sitting there waiting for the next shot so I could absolve myself.

When the hunting was done he'd walk back with me to town, trotting alongside, until we arrived at the bridge. There he would stop and sit down and nothing I did would make him come farther. I tried waiting him out to see where he would go but when it was obvious that I wasn't going to leave he merely lay down and went to sleep, or turned and started back into the woods, looking back to see if we were going hunting again.

Once I left him, crossed the bridge and then hid in the back of a building and watched. He stayed until I was out of sight and then turned and trotted north away from the bridge along the river. There were no houses in that direction, at least on the far side of the river, and I watched him until he disappeared into the woods. I was no wiser than I had been.

The rest of his life was a mystery and would remain so for thirty years. But when we were together we became fast friends, at least on my part.

I would cook an extra egg sandwich for Ike and when the flights weren't coming we would "talk". That is to say, I would talk, tell him all my troubles, and he would sit, his enormous head sometimes resting on my knee, his huge brown eyes looking up at me while I petted him and rattled on.

On the weekends when I stayed out, I would construct a lean-to and make a fire, and he would curl up on the edge of my blanket. Many mornings I would awaken to find him under the frost-covered blanket with me, sound asleep, my arm thrown over him, his breath rumbling against my side.

It seemed like there'd always been an Ike in my life and then one morning he wasn't there and I never saw him again. I tried to find him. I would wait for him in the mornings by the bridge, but he never showed again. I thought he might have gotten hit by a car, or his owners moved away. I mourned him and missed him. But I did not learn what happened to him for thirty years.

I grew and went into the crazy parts of life, army and those other mistakes a young man could make. I grew older and got back into dogs, this time sled dogs, and ran the Iditarod race across Alaska. After my first run I came back to Minnesota with slides of the race to show to all the people who had supported me. A sporting goods store had been one of my sponsors and I gave a public slide show of the race one evening.

There was an older man sitting in a wheelchair and I saw that when I told a story of how Cookie, my lead dog, had saved my life his eyes teared up and he nodded quietly.

When the event was over he wheeled up to me and shook my hands.

"I had a dog like your Cookie – a dog that saved my life."

"Oh – did you run sleds?"

He shook his head. "No. Not like that. I lived up in Twin Forks when I was young and was drafted to serve in the Korean War. I had a Labrador that I raised and hunted with, and left him when I went away. I was gone just under a year; I got wounded and lost the use of my legs. When I came back from the hospital he was waiting there and he spent the rest of his life by my side. I would have gone crazy without him. I'd sit for hours and talk to him and he would listen quietly . . . it was so sad. He loved to hunt and I never hunted again." He faded off and his eyes were moist again. "I still miss him . . ."

I looked at him, then out of the window of the sporting goods store. It was spring and the snow was melting outside but I was seeing a fall and a boy and a Lab sitting in a duck blind. Twin Forks, he'd said –

and the Korean War. The time was right, and the place, and the dog.

"Your dog," I said. "Was he named Ike?"

He smiled and nodded. "Why, yes – but how . . . did you know him?"

There was a soft spring rain starting and the window misted with it. That was why Ike had not come back. He had another job.

"Yes," I said, turning to him. "He was my friend . . ."

Katzenfell

Christobel Mattingley

I never did like the feel of fur. To me it seems eerie somehow. It always made me squeamish to think of the skin of an animal long dead, still transmitting life and warmth.

And when my mother wore her silver fox fur around her neck, I tried not to look at its little feet dangling from her shoulders – feet that had left their footprints on the snow in a far-off land. I tried not to look at its pointed ears which once had heard the wind's songs. And I did not look at all at its eyes or nose, which now were only glass and leather, but which once had seen and smelled sights and scents I would never know.

I vowed to myself that I would never wear fur – in a coat or a cape, a cap or even a collar. But I did. And a strange thing happened.

It was in Bavaria. And I believe that anything could happen in Bavaria. Beautiful Bavaria, the very

163

heart of Europe. Crowned with mountains whose snow-white peaks exchange secrets with the wind and create mysteries with the clouds. Clothed with deep forests where deer and wild boar live. Studded with villages whose wide-eaved houses and onion-domed churches seem to have come straight out of fairytales.

I had come to study in a famous old Bavarian city and I was living in a tiny room in the garden of the house of an old lady. One night close to Christmas I was coming home late from the library, when I slipped on the icy path. I fell with a force that jarred me right up my spine, and when I pulled myself up carefully and gathered my books which had scattered in the snow, the pain was so great it was all I could do to make my way to my room.

Slowly I peeled off my wet clothes and crawled under the bedcovers. But sleep would not come to blot out my pain and I lay awake in the bitter darkness for hour after hour. Then in the distance I heard a wailing screech which glazed my eyes and froze my fingernails. The sound came closer, closer, until my ears were aching with it. There was a hideous crescendo. Then suddenly it stopped. I lay exhausted, in fearful silence as piercing as my pain.

Sleep came then and when I woke the midwinter sun was probing at the window, making freckles on

the wall through the lace curtains. It shone on the
icicles hanging from the eave so that they looked like
diamond pencils, and I was lying wondering what
sort of a story one could write with such a pencil,
when a shadow fell on the window.

It was my landlady, a kindly old soul, who nevertheless kept a watchful eye on my comings and
goings, as landladies do. She had come to investigate
why, by midday, I had not left for the library. When
she found me in bed, she tutted and clucked and
muttered a mouthful of Bavarian, a dialect I could
not understand. Then, after plumping up my pillow,
she pulled her shawl over her head and left.

I was dozing when she came back, carrying an old

pewter pot from which steam was curling with smells I could not recognize. When she produced a long-handled spoon, I remembered the saying about supping with the devil, and as she lifted the first spoonful to my mouth, I suddenly wanted to know what it was she was giving me.

As if she read my thoughts she laughed and said in a sing-song voice, "The breast of a hen, the liver of a pig, the heart of an onion." She went on chanting a long list of other ingredients as she fed me the broth she had brewed. "Kräuter und Würze, Kümmel und Kamille, Pilze und Petersilie, Schnittlauch, Knoblauch." The German words seemed to weave a spell about my mind as the clear golden broth warmed and soothed my aching body.

She drained the pot to the very last drop of the herb-rich concoction, patted my bedcovers and left, and I slid easily then into a restful sleep.

She woke me when she came the third time. She was carrying a copper kettle from which she poured a deep red liquid into a squat copper mug. I caught my breath on the strong spicy vapours and she smiled and said, "Zimt und Zucker und Zitrone, and the wine must be red, always red." I sipped and the potion ran through me like fire.

She refilled the mug and stood over me while I drank it. Then from under her shawl she produced a soft shapeless bundle.

"Katzenfell," she said, and I wondered if I had heard aright. But now she was unrolling it, holding it out. And there was no doubt.

It was the skin of a cat.

A large cat, a very large cat. Dark grey, almost black with tabby markings of deep burnt orange.

"Fritz," she said fondly and stroked it as if it were still alive.

I felt sick.

"Warm," she said, wrapped it round her back and tied it to her with long red strings. Then she took it off, nodded to me and laid it at the foot of my bed.

She meant me to wear it!

My skin prickled. I closed my eyes so that I did not have to look at it.

She chuckled, poured the dregs from the kettle into my mug, put it into my hands and left. I swallowed the last mouthful, which was thick with cinnamon, and fell at once into a curious kind of sleep, where the big feather bedcover seemed to wrap me round like yeasty dough and the pain was slicing through my vertebrae like a knife.

How long I slept I do not know, but it was dark when a movement in the room and a glimmering sort of light woke me. I thought at first it was the old woman again, and called, "Grüss Gott!", the traditional Bavarian greeting. But there was no answer and the glimmer disappeared.

I wanted to turn on the light, but I could not move, either for fear or for the pain in my back, I did not know which. I lay in the dark, paralysed, conscious only of the furry shape at my feet, hating it, wishing it would go away. But it did not, and its presence seemed to send little electric shocks up and down my spine.

I shivered. Could there be any truth in the old saying that cats have nine lives? Fritz had obviously been no ordinary cat. But then, and I consoled myself, it must have taken him all of nine lives to grow to such an immense size.

The skin which the old woman had held up was headless. But now there was an occasional golden glint again at the end of the bed. I felt quite certain that I was being watched. Watched by Fritz.

It was not possible, I told myself.

But then I remembered some of the Bavarian folktales I had read. And I knew with chill certainty that strange things could happen at midwinter. I broke into an icy sweat and waited.

I found then that my feet, for no reason, seemed to be growing warm, and a vibration was running up my legs. Suddenly, without knowing how or why I did it, I was wrapping the cat fur around me. And in the darkness I was beginning to see the outline of objects in the room, the window, the door. I yawned and stretched, and a ripple of power flowed through me. All my pain had disappeared.

"So, now we are in business," Fritz said. "Pleased to meet you." He gave a chuckle which reverberated through me. "My old woman is a knowing one. Yes," he rumbled in satisfaction, "a very knowing one. She can pick a likely body."

I got out of bed and moved to the door, walking more easily, more gracefully than I had ever walked before in my life. Fritz was purring, a low hypnotic sound which seemed to take possession of my chest and my ears, my mind and my whole body.

In the distance there was a long screeching wail, like the sound I had heard the night before. I stiffened. Fritz spat. "The fools," he hissed. "Have they forgotten that I was king of the cats for nine years? Do they think they can take over my territory so easily? We'll show them," he snarled. And I felt my heart beating fast.

As we sprang through the door, Fritz let out a howl which echoed and re-echoed off the nearby buildings, sending icicles shattering to the path. We bounded across the garden and in one leap we were up on a wall abutting the old woman's house. I felt my muscles flex as we crouched for the next longer leap across to a narrow window ledge.

We pressed against the glass and Fritz crooned softly. As a hump in the bed beneath the window moved and muttered in reply, I knew we were looking into the old woman's room.

Then we were off again, up, up, and on to the rooftops. "I have three scores to settle tonight. And we'll deal with the cats first," Fritz said. "We'll put the fear of Fritz back where it belongs."

We prowled along the ridges of the roofs, peering, prying, leaping from ledge to ledge, listening, looking, skirting clusters of chimney pots gathered together like gossiping old women. We came to a modern block of flats, which seemed rather out of place among the old steep-gabled houses.

We paused. "Never did like that building," Fritz said. We looked along the symmetrical rows of staring windows blankly opening on wide balconies, so different from the higgledy-piggledy dormers and attics winking under their tiled eyelids.

Fritz said slowly, "I have a feeling the trouble is in that box. A pedigreed Pandora in the penthouse maybe. Let's see. It won't take long."

He walked disdainfully along the outer edge of the balustrade. "To think that they pulled down perfectly good houses to build this! You couldn't imagine anything more boring. No risk, no challenge. It's an insult to every self-respecting cat. It only encourages them to let their life insurance policies lapse."

We came to the flat roof which was set out like a garden, with trees in tubs and plants in pots. A table with a furled umbrella and several chairs were folded against a wall.

"Yes," Fritz repeated, "there's a chocolate box cat sending out signals from here, and every tom in the district is coming to fight over her. Pussyfeet!" His tone was scathing. "In my young days it was an adventure to look for a lady on the rooftops. But this! We might as well be walking in the town square."

Through the glass door of the apartment we glimpsed a simpering fluffy white Persian with a blue satin bow around her neck.

"I told you so," Fritz said.

While we watched she uttered a low call which was at once answered with strident cries from every quarter. Fritz, with the experience of an old campaigner, ignored the lady, and we took up a strategic position facing all comers, in the shadow of the terrace furniture.

The chorus of cats was coming closer and closer. The white cat was preening herself and smirking as her first suitor came over the balustrade.

He never knew what happened to him. Neither did the next cat, nor the following. Fritz was striking and cuffing, sending cats flying in all directions, and the blanket of night was suddenly rent by shrieks and howls and the crashing of pots and furniture, as the terrified toms tried to escape the silent fury which attacked them.

Fritz caterwauled triumphantly as the last vanquished intruder on his territory tumbled ignominiously out of sight. "They won't be back in a hurry." Then he turned on the vain little Persian who was looking hopefully for the victor from safety behind the glass. "Get back to your velvet cushion where you belong," he sneered, "if you're too scared to get into the act. Calendar cat!"

The white cat gave an outraged mew and a light flashed on in the room. A woman in a velvet dressing gown appeared. She picked up the white cat and exclaimed, "My poor little precious! Did those nasty alley cats frighten my baby? Hans!" she called.

A sleepy man in pyjamas joined her unwillingly.

"Look at this!" she said to him. "See what those wretched tom cats have done to our terrace! They've broken all my potplants and they've absolutely terrified my poor little Blossom. She's trembling, aren't you, darling?" She cuddled the white cat. "We'll just have to find another apartment in a better neighbourhood. I've always said this area isn't good enough for Blossom. All these ill-bred alley cats from those old houses. It's like living in the slums."

I could feel Fritz's fur bristling. He let out such an angry screech that the woman jumped and clutched her husband, dropping the white cat as she did so. It fell in a mewling heap and the man, stepping forward to hold his wife, trod on it. The white cat squealed and sprang up the curtains, knocking over the lampshade and a tall vase of flowers as it went.

Fritz laughed until my belly ached as we made our way past the overturned table and umbrella, pausing on the balustrade while Fritz gloated over the panic and chaos we had created. "So, we've sent them packing," he said with satisfaction. "That was a good warming-up exercise. Now we'll deal with the dog."

The dog in question was a bad-tempered brute, which did not mind its own business, so Fritz gave me to understand. He did not tell me exactly what the dog had done, but obviously there had been an incident which still rankled with him.

We approached the dog's yard and halted on the wall in the shadow of a large linden tree. Down below there was the chink of a chain and a whimper as the dog twitched in a dream. "He's remembering me," Fritz said. "You see." He gave a low spitting hiss and the dog jerked awake with a yelp.

I had to admire Fritz's tactics. We stayed out of sight – or could it be that we were invisible? – but

Fritz made sure the dog was aware of our presence, taunting him so that the dog was barking in a frenzy of frustration.

A window opened and a man stuck his head out. "Quiet!" he shouted. "Lie down!" He slammed the window.

"Quiet! Lie down!" Fritz hissed, and the dog jumped up and began to bark again.

This time the door on to the yard opened and the man came out. "What's up?" he asked. The dog barked frantically and the man looked round the yard. He flashed a torch into every corner and up along the walls. The dog barked furiously as the torchlight flickered over where we were. But the man saw nothing and turned off the torch.

"You're imagining things," he told the dog crossly. "Dreaming. Now go to sleep and let people do the same. Darn dog," he grumbled as he returned to the house.

Fritz waited a moment to give the man time to go back to bed. Then he called in a low sing-song voice, "Darn dog is dreaming. Darn dog is dreaming."

The dog was nearly beside himself. The chain rattled as he pranced and jumped, trying to reach his tormentor, and he barked so desperately that windows began to open in nearby houses, and people began shouting abuse at him. The insults doubled when his owner appeared again, as the neighbours yelled complaints as well as bawling at the dog.

Fritz laughed under his breath as the master began to berate the dog. "He's got the dog he deserves," he said. "A man who doesn't trust his dog can't control him." He listened for a moment with great satisfaction, then made his final contribution to the hullabaloo he had begun – a nerve-tingling squall that silenced everybody, including the dog.

Fritz chuckled. "The dog at odds with his master, the master at odds with the dog and the neighbours as well. A neat revenge on an old enemy," he complimented himself.

"Now for the last account." Fritz's tone was not pleasant to hear. "That boy will be longing for daylight after we've called on him." He said no more, and as we bounded over the roofs, I wondered about the victim of our next visit. He must have teased Fritz at some time. Maybe he had made a habit of it. Whatever it was that he had done, there was no doubt in my mind that he was about to pay heavily for it. But just how heavily I still did not know.

Snow was floating down like feathers, masking paths, filling in footprints, smothering sounds, spreading fresh covers over the existing drifts, which lay in puffs and humps like gigantic eiderdowns over the roofs. And the moonlight threw weird shadows over the white world.

Fritz climbed purposefully towards a high dormer window and I knew we were approaching our goal. We jumped on to the ledge and stared in at the window. In a bed below a boy lay sleeping. The boy. I could feel Fritz making him conscious of his presence, needling him through dreams and half remembered happenings. Then suddenly, sharply, the boy awoke, uneasily aware of something strange, something about to happen.

The boy's eyes darted round the room, searching the shadows for unknown shapes, and when his gaze was turned away from the window, Fritz drew his claws down the glass in a sound that set my teeth on edge. The boy looked out quickly, but Fritz was crouching low behind the rim of snow along the window-sill. Then, as soon as he turned away again, Fritz repeated his action.

The boy sat up and looked out once more. He was shaken, but still in command of himself. Fritz waited. He was very good at waiting. Finally the boy lay down again, and pulled the cover over himself.

Fritz waited a little longer. Then he let out the most horrendous shriek I had heard him utter. It seemed to summon every grotesque fear one might have ever had, from all the hidden corners of the

176

mind. The bedcover was trembling and for a long while the boy did not dare to pull it off his head. The moon went behind a cloud and the snow began to fall more heavily. Gradually Fritz's fur was covered with a coat of clinging flakes. But he waited without moving.

Just as the boy began to peer out at last, the moon shone forth with a startling brilliance. Fritz stretched then in one long slow movement and stood up on his hind legs. The reflections of his eyes glowed on the glass. The boy stared in horror and I knew what he was seeing.

"A ghost!" he yelled hoarsely. "It's a ghost!" He jumped from his bed and we could hear his panic-stricken footsteps thudding down the stairs.

Fritz laughed. A sinister laugh. The boy's terror was the breath of life to him. He said, "That's taught him not to tease the king of the cats. He'll remember Fritz when every tooth in his gums has rotted and every hair on his scalp has fallen out."

He stretched his claws. "I'm hungry. I rather fancy a little snack – a nice plump pigeon, or better still a pair," he added politely for my benefit.

We headed for the church and walked the dizzy distance along the roof of the nave to the tower. Fritz looked up at the clock. "Not much time," he muttered. "We'll have to hurry."

We jumped up on to a parapet and began to stalk towards a huddle of pigeons sleeping beneath the clock. We sprang and I was sure that Fritz's claws had found their mark, because I saw a couple of pigeon feathers float by. But then there was a thunderous booming which shook me to the core and all I knew was that the snow was sliding and I was falling, falling into darkness.

It was midday when I woke, and although the sun was shining into the room I was cold, because my feather bedcovers had slipped and lay on the floor like a snowdrift from a roof. Only where the cat fur was still wrapped around my back was I warm. I touched the fur gingerly and it seemed to send a shock through me. I stretched and felt my body lithe and completely free of pain.

"Fritz," I said. I still felt possessed and the memories of the night were vivid.

Could it have happened? Or was it a dream?

I walked to the door. The new snow was dazzling in the sun, fresh, pure, unmarked. Except for the footprints of a very large cat coming to my door.

I was still staring at them, when the old woman came out of her house. She was carrying a tray. She greeted me with a knowing smile and set the tray on my table. She pulled out a chair for me and patted the fur as I sat down. "Fritz's favourite," she said. I thought she meant the milk, which was in a shallow pottery drinking bowl. But she took the lid off a small earthenware cooking pot.

There, floating in a rich brown gravy, was a pair of plump-breasted pigeons.

The Wire and
the Woodpecker

Noël Douglas Evans

From my window I could see the world. It ran to distant mountains that sat hazy and dimly blue on the horizon. Somewhere in the middle was a huge lake of deep blue water. I couldn't see it but I knew it was there. From the edge of my bed I could just glimpse a section of our huge mountain that sat grandly behind our house. Down below was a field full of cane, light and tanned from the everlasting sun. From our garden, the sun would rise gradually out of sight and into the distance. A huge tree stood to one side of the house, a telephone wire stretching from its branches and looping across so that it barely missed my open window. Shadows would dance around my room as the sun moved over the horizon with the leaves and wire creating strange shapes on the wall. This was home. My home in Africa, where the smells and noises are the strongest and loudest I've ever experienced. And from one of those noises I found myself my special friend.

At first, I thought it was someone knocking on my door, but one morning it was so loud that I edged down to the end of my bed and, peeking through the net curtain, saw the most beautiful, crested bird tapping on my window. Now and then it would stop and cock its head to one side and then tap some more. Without disturbing it, I unscrambled myself from the bedding, pulled a sheet out from under and slipped on to the floor. But when I reappeared at the window, it had gone. I waited for a while but it didn't come back. I so wanted to see this bird again! To be so close to it and see the curve of its beak and the lines of its feathers was fascinating. Maybe it was a woodpecker of some sort!

Later that first day, I found a book on birds at school. It was sticky and horrible with jam and other unknown substances and some of the pages were stuck together. It was a slow process during lunch break. While everyone played outside, I sat behind in the silent classroom and fingered my way through the book. My friends thought I was crazy. It was difficult to explain to them the discovery trail I was on. Then, suddenly I had found it. Staring up at me from the page, it looked just like the bird at my window: big, bold and beautiful. I stared closely at the picture. It wasn't a woodpecker after all but an African Hoopoe. It did many of the same things as a woodpecker, though. Like a woodpecker, it would nest in a hole in the tree and tap the bark for worms and other food using its beak. I had already nick-named him Woody so it pleased me to know there were many similarities. Even his colouring was woody. Reading further, a strange sort of sensation came over me. It was a feeling of inner knowledge. Learning about the inner secrets of another animal was rather like learning a new language. Communication. Yes, that's what it was all about. Imagine how wonderful it would be to be able to speak to a bird! The school-bell sounded and I suddenly felt quite silly: communicate with a bird, how ridiculous!

By the second week of spring there was still no reappearance of Woody. I began to think it was all a dream, that it didn't actually happen. All the food I left on the window ledge was being stolen by marauding ants. And when finally I heard the tapping again, it was softer and more distant, so I didn't recognize it at first. "It had to be," I thought to myself. I was almost afraid I wouldn't hear it again, but the tapping continued, stopping and starting at irregular intervals. This time I took special care to keep quiet, fearing that the slightest jerky move or foreign sound would scare it off. The bed creaked a little, the sheets shuffled, but on the cold floor I crept silently to the window. Journeying slowly across the floor as my eyes kept level with the bottom of the window frame was hard on my knees. I thought it would probably be better if I approached it from the corner, using the open curtain as a camouflage. It felt like ages, squatting underneath the sill. There was no sign of Woody but the tapping was still there. Without moving, I rolled my eyes around. Yes. There he was! He was perched close on the wire, tapping on the enamel terminal of the telephone pole. Then he dropped down to the sill, right in front of my nose and picked up one of the last pieces of dry bread. For a moment I thought he was going to dart off as he eyeballed me first with one eye, then the other. Returning to the wire, he rested the bread on the white terminal and picked at it.

And that's how it all started. Every night, I would leave some bread, or raisin loaf on my window sill. I even tried fancy things like choc dip or crunched up cornflakes with sticky sugar and stuck it to the enamel terminals. Woody would tap on both, creating a tune, just like that movie, *Close Encounters of the Third Kind*: as if he was giving some sort of friendly message to us humans! I found that now I

184

could get really close to him and one day, he came to
see me in the evening as the sun was sinking and his
beak was all brown or black. I watched for a while
from inside, before reaching out slowly to the wire.
He stopped tapping for a moment and watched as my
hand went round one of the terminals. It felt squidgy
and soft, even sticky. I thought that it must have
been the chocolate or sugar that had got wedged. As
my fingers felt around the top, Woody started
tapping me. It was such a shock, I leapt back in
surprise and Woody took off. Looking closely at my
tapped fingers, I could still see the marks from his
beak. But that wasn't at all what I was concerned
about. The sticky substance wasn't chocolate or

sugar or anything edible. It was a sort of resin or sticky rubber, and it smelt awful too. It must have been coming from the terminal. Now I had a problem. I didn't want to change anything which would frighten Woody away, but he couldn't go on dipping into this substance. I was sure it would make him ill.

Dinner was always early during the week and especially during school term. My sister and I would sit with Mom and Dad and listen to their gossip of the day. Mom would smile and feed us, but generally it was the time when we were seen but not expected to be heard. In those days we had an old Bakelite phone. It was black and very heavy. We used to complain about it constantly, asking for a modern, cordless phone like some of our friends had. Dad would just grin and tell us that the big, old Bakelite stopped us from spending too much time on the phone as it was so heavy. Dad thought it was a huge joke, but we didn't think so, of course. So that evening when they started talking about the phone I listened carefully. Dad spoke to Mom through slurps of soup.

"You know that crackle I was complaining about on the phone?" Mom nodded in response. "Well now it's this irritating tapping. I feel as though I'm back in the army listening to some ridiculous morse code. It almost is, you know. I started writing down the letters but none made any sense. I'm going to get the telephone people in to have a look at it. I have noticed that the wire is very low, and dropping through the tree."

I couldn't help it. I coughed and spluttered my soup all over the place. Mom patted me on the back, thinking I was choking. "You alright, son?"

Now the whole world had collapsed. Well that's how it felt to me. Woody's clever antics had backfired on him, and now we had to look forward to the telephone men. The news couldn't be worse. It was one thing to try and solve Woody's sticky problem with that awful substance, but it was another to upset the whole communication development that was currently in progress.

I thought of everything: writing a letter to the telephone people, pretending I was Dad, and cancelling the appointment; blocking them off at the road and telling them they had the wrong address. But there seemed to be nothing I could do.

The only other thing was to report sick and stay at home the day the telephone repairmen arrived. At least I could try to do *something*. Meanwhile, the tapping on the phone continued and everybody was getting really annoyed. Trying to talk to someone on the phone was proving to be impossible with this continual *tap tap tap*. Finally, the telephone line just went dead. No amount of thumping and shouting made the phone come back to life.

The day the men in blue with ladders and helmets arrived, I tried to capture Woody, but he thought it was just a game. He just hopped further down the wire and pecked at my hand. He was quick too. The food in my hand was taken every time. "Listen," I said, "You've got to get off this wire for a moment." But he just looked at me and tapped at the wire. Eventually, I was forced to leave for school. Woody followed me to the end of the garden, finding the most fragile part of a branch to balance on.

I dreaded coming home, wondering what I was going to see. From a distance, it didn't look too bad. I could still see a telephone wire, and the tree didn't look any different at all. But when I looked through my window, it was a different story. The tree had a big hole in it and its leaves and branches had been cut away. The wire went straight through the middle. My heart sank. It no longer drooped down by my window. It had been raised so high I wondered if it was still connected to the house. And there seemed to be no sign of Woody, none at all.

Jonathan, my friend from school, came around the next day. We invented some fantastic games together. One was a moving target we had rigged up at the bottom of the garden. We prided ourselves on being the best air rifle shooters in our school. That day we held our own practice competition. We were very strict with ourselves when it came to firing our pellet guns. We were taught never to point them at anyone, ever! Accidents can happen, so keeping the possibility to a minimum was important. The rifles would be taken away from us if we were irresponsible. So we made sure we were very careful indeed.

The reason why they were taken away from us this fateful day was rather unfair. It was all a terrible accident. I had looked back briefly at the house, gazing absent-mindedly really, while we re-set everything. As we were reloading, one of the rifles fired into the air. Luckily it didn't hit either of us. It's strange how you remember everything in slow motion.

I remember seeing Woody clambering along the wire from the tree. It had never occurred to me that he could have been living in the tree.

Then *BANG*!

I heard the pellet hit the tin guttering against the roof, but not before I saw Woody flutter madly, and then crash dive to the ground. Screaming, I scrambled up the embankment and ran as fast as I could. I couldn't see anything on the grass or on the pavement. Then something caught my eye in the flower bed. Woody lay there, limp. A huge lump welled up in my throat. Jonathan apologized but how could he know what would happen. There was my special feathered friend lying dead, all because of our stupid guns!

I picked Woody up carefully and with both hands carried him inside. I gently laid him on a towel on my bed, making sure his wings weren't twisted. I just stood and stared. "What a beautiful bird," I whispered as I stroked him softly. There was no blood or anything. No evidence of a wound. His body still felt warm and I thought I could feel his heart beat ever so slightly.

Strangely, there seemed to be a lot of commotion outside by the tree. I peeked through the window. I glanced back at Woody and quickly went outside to investigate. A hole in the tree seemed to have life in it and sure enough when I heaved myself on to the first branch and looked in, I saw babies. The mother bird squealed and tapped around me furiously. The babies looked like they were ready to fly.

"This must be Woody's family!" I shouted out loud. Leaping from the tree and back to my bedroom only took a moment, but in that time something had changed.

Woody was no longer on the towel!

He was nowhere. Maybe Jonathan had taken him. No, that wasn't possible. He had gone.

But something at the window caught my attention. It was a movement silhouetted against the sky. Woody was perched on the window sill! He pecked at the window twice and then was gone. It seemed like ages before I gulped air into my lungs and blinked. My eyes felt dry so I rubbed them and I blinked again several times before focusing on the wire.

They had gone!

Every day, I had a look out of my window. I waited some mornings for the familiar tapping but, sadly, all was quiet. It was strange that you could miss an animal so much.

I thought, as the months turned into a year, that I would never see him again. Spring had come round again. The tree had grown its leaves, the wire had dropped lower to the window and the smell of a new African dawn breathed in through the curtains. I was by the phone when it rang. It was for Dad, but as I put my hand over the mouthpiece to call him, I heard the sound. It was the tapping! I was so excited I just put the phone down and ran.

Outside on the wire, right up against the two new porcelain telephone terminals, was Woody. Tapping on the enamel, he looked at me and then tapped some more. Time for feeding, I thought, as I rushed to the kitchen for some bread.

191

Snapshot of a Dog

James Thurber

I ran across a dim photograph of him the other day, going through some old things. He's been dead twenty-five years. His name was Rex (my two brothers and I named him when we were in our early teens) and he was a bull terrier. "An American bull terrier," we used to say proudly; none of your English bulls. He had one brindle eye that sometimes made him look like a clown and sometimes reminded you of a politician with derby hat and cigar. The rest of him was white except for a brindle saddle that always seemed to be slipping off and a brindle stocking on a hind leg. Nevertheless, there was a nobility about him. He was big and muscular and beautifully made. He never lost his dignity even when trying to accomplish the extravagant tasks my brothers and myself used to set for him.

One of these was the bringing of a ten-foot wooden rail into the yard through the back gate. We would throw it out into the alley and tell him to go get it. Rex was as powerful as a wrestler, and there were not many things that he couldn't manage somehow to get hold of with his great jaws and lift or drag to wherever he wanted to put them, or wherever we wanted them put. He could catch the rail at the balance and lift it clear of the ground and trot with great confidence towards the gate. Of course, since the gate was only four feet wide or so, he couldn't bring the rail in broadside. He found that out when he got a few terrific jolts, but he wouldn't give up. He finally figured out how to do it, by dragging the rail, holding on to one end, growling. He got a great, wagging satisfaction out of his work. We used to bet kids who had never seen Rex in action that he could catch a baseball thrown as high as they could throw it. He almost never let us down. Rex could hold a baseball with ease in his mouth, in one cheek, as if it were a chew of tobacco.

He was a tremendous fighter, but he never started fights. I don't believe he liked to get into them, despite the fact that he came from a line of fighters. He never went for another dog's throat, but for one of its ears (that teaches a dog a lesson), and he would get his grip, close his eyes, and hold on. He could hold on for hours. His longest fight lasted from dusk until almost pitch-dark, one Sunday. It was fought in

East Main Street in Columbus with a large, snarly nondescript that belonged to a big black man. When Rex finally got his ear grip the brief whirlwind of snarling turned to screeching. It was frightening to listen to and to watch. The man boldly picked the dogs up somehow and began swinging them round his head, and finally let them fly like a hammer throw, but although they landed ten feet away with a great plump, Rex still held on.

The two dogs eventually worked their way to the middle of the car tracks, and two to three streetcars were held up by the fight. A motorman tried to pry Rex's jaws open with a switch rod; somebody lighted a fire and made a torch of a stick and held that to Rex's tail, but he paid no attention. In the end, all the residents and storekeepers in the neighbourhood were on hand, shouting this, suggesting that.

Rex's joy of battle, when battle was joined, was almost tranquil. He had a kind of pleasant expression during fights, not a vicious one, his eyes closed in what would have seemed to be sleep had it not been for the turmoil of the struggle. The Oak Street Fire Department finally had to be sent for – I don't know why nobody thought of it sooner. Five or six pieces of apparatus arrived, followed by a battalion chief. A hose was attached and a powerful stream of water was turned on the dogs. Rex held on for several moments more while the torrent buffeted him about like a log in a freshnet. He was a hundred yards away from where the fight started when he finally let go.

The story of the Homeric fight got all around town, and some of our relatives looked upon the incident as a blot on the family name. They insisted that we get rid of Rex, but we were happy with him, and nobody could have made us give him up. We would have left town with him first, along any road there was to go. It would have been different, perhaps, if he'd ever started fights, or looked for trouble. But he had a gentle disposition. He never bit a person in the ten

strenuous years that he lived, nor even growled at anyone except prowlers. He killed cats, that is true, but quickly and neatly and without especial malice, the way men kill certain animals. It was the only thing he did that we could never cure him of doing. He never killed, or even chased, a squirrel. I don't know why. He had his own philosophy about such things. He never ran barking after wagons or automobiles. He didn't seem to see the idea in pursuing something you couldn't catch, or something you couldn't do anything with even if you did catch it. A wagon was one of the things he couldn't tug along with his mighty jaws, and he knew it. Wagons, therefore, were not a part of his world.

Swimming was his favourite recreation. The first time he ever saw a body of water (Alum Creek), he trotted nervously along the steep bank for a while, fell to barking wildly, and finally plunged in from a height of eight feet or more. I shall always remember that shining, virgin dive. Then he swam upstream and back just for the pleasure of it, like a man. It was fun to see him battle upstream against a stiff current, struggling and growling every foot of the way. He had as much fun in the water as any person I have known. You didn't have to throw a stick in the water to get him to go in. Of course, he would bring back a stick to you if you did throw one in. He would even have brought back a piano if you had thrown one in.

That reminds me of the night, way after midnight, when he went a-roving in the light of the moon and brought back a small chest of drawers that he found somewhere – how far from the house nobody ever knew; since it was Rex, it could easily have been half a mile. There were no drawers in the chest when he got it home, and it wasn't a good one – he hadn't taken it out of anybody's house; it was just an old cheap piece that somebody had abandoned on a trash heap. Still, it was something he wanted, probably because it presented a nice problem in transportation. It tested his mettle. We first knew about his achievement when, deep in the night, we heard him trying to get the chest up on to the porch. It sounded as if two or three people were trying to tear the house down. We came downstairs and turned on the porch light. Rex was on the top step trying to pull the thing up, but it had caught somehow and he was just holding his own till dawn if we hadn't helped him. The next day we carted the chest miles away and threw it out. If we had thrown it out in a nearby alley he would have brought it home again, as a small token of his integrity in such matters. After all, he had been taught to carry heavy wooden objects about, and he was proud of his prowess.

I am glad Rex never saw a trained police dog jump.

He was just an amateur jumper himself, but the most daring and tenacious I have ever seen. He would take on any fence we pointed out to him. Six feet was easy for him, and he could do eight by making a tremendous leap and hauling himself over finally by his paws, grunting and straining; but he lived and died without knowing that twelve- and sixteen-foot walls were too much for him. Frequently, after letting him try to go over one for a while, we would have to carry him home. He would never have given up trying.

There was in his world no such thing as the impossible. Even death couldn't beat him down. He died, it is true, but only, as one of his admirers said, after "straight-arming the death angel" for more than an hour. Late one afternoon he wandered home, too slowly and too uncertainly to be the Rex that had trotted briskly homeward up our avenue for ten years. I think we all knew when he came through the gate that he was dying. He had apparently taken a terrible beating, probably from the owner of some dog that he had got into a fight with. His head and body were scarred. His heavy collar with the teeth marks of many a battle on it was awry; some of the big brass studs in it were sprung loose from the leather. He licked at our hands and, staggering, fell, but got up again. We could see that he was looking for someone. One of his three masters was not home. He did not get home for an hour. During that time the bull terrier fought against death as he had fought against the cold strong current of Alum Creek, as he had fought to climb twelve-foot walls. When the person he was waiting for did come through the gate, whistling, ceasing to whistle, Rex walked a few wobbly paces towards him, touched his hand with his muzzle, and fell down again. This time he didn't get up.

The Great
Elephant Chase

Gillian Cross

Tad and Cissie are determined to release Khush the elephant from his imprisonment. He is being held by Mr Jackson, who Tad now works for. Mr Jackson pretended that he bought Khush before the elephant's real owner (and Cissie's father) Michael Keenan was killed in a train accident. But Cissie's plan – to sneak Khush out at night – is fraught with danger ...

At the livery stable, Tad huddled uneasily in his rickety shed. Outside in the darkness, the dogs barked and the horses stamped and whinnied. He knew he should sleep, but his eyes refused to stay closed. His mind was churning miserably, full of Cissie's instructions.

Then, at midnight, he opened the door to check

that Khush was all right and saw – nothing. Not even Khush, although he could hear him munching, very close. The yard was invisible. Fog had slid down on to Pittsburgh, writhing into every alley and narrow back yard and carrying the dirty smell of coal smoke wherever it went.

Tad closed his eyes and leaned against the doorpost. He hadn't realized, until that moment, how much Cissie's plan had frightened him. But now the fog had made it impossible. He turned back into the shed, wriggled under some dusty straw and fell asleep.

Two hours later, Cissie woke him up. She crouched close to his face, holding a lantern over him as she shook his shoulder.

"Why are you asleep? I told you to be ready!"

"How did you ever—?" Tad blinked up at her. "Has the fog cleared?"

"No, it hasn't. I had to follow the rivers to be sure of finding you. I've been all the way round the Point in the dark."

Tad didn't know what she meant, but he could feel how cold she was. She picked up his boots and dropped them on top of him.

"Put these on! We have to get started!"

"But the fog—"

"The fog is wonderful! Better than anything we could have planned. Come *on*!" She put down the lantern and tried to push his feet into his boots.

"But—"

"There's no time to argue!"

Tad pulled on the boots and crept after her, out into the yard. She threw her shawl over the lantern and they had to feel their way round the walls to where Khush was chained, moving towards the sound of his shuffling feet.

It was Tad who put his hand on the iron ring. Khush's chain ran through it, and both ends were locked to the metal anklet round his back leg. The links of the chain felt cold and damp under Tad's fingers.

And Mr Jackson had the key.

Cissie's hand met Tad's, running the other way up the chain, and he heard her sigh with relief.

"Only one leg chained. That's good. Hold on to the ring, and don't let it fall when it comes loose."

In the main stable yard, the dogs caught the faint sound of her voice and threw themselves into a frenzy of barking. But Khush rumbled contentedly and scraped his feet over the cobbles.

"Steady there," Cissie crooned, feeling her way along the chain towards him. "Not yet."

He rumbled again as she reached him, and she

202

murmured very softly, so that Tad barely heard.

"Move up. Move up, there."

The chain tautened and Khush strained at it for a moment. Then he let it go slack.

Cissie hissed more fiercely. "Move up, Khush!"

This time he stayed quite still, except for a puzzled snort.

"I've got to get him moving," Cissie whispered. "Where's the bullhook?"

Tad fumbled back to the shed and found the short, thick stick with the steel tip. Cissie snatched it out of his hands and gestured back towards the ring. "Don't let that drop. And watch yourself. He won't be pleased."

Dimly, through the fog, Tad saw her swing the stick and jab forwards as she hissed her order again.

"Move *up*, Khush!"

There was a roar of rage that sent the dogs wild, and the chain jerked so hard that Tad felt the great iron ring shift in the wall.

Cissie jabbed again. "Move up!"

This time, the roar was ear-splitting. Khush heaved with all his strength and the iron ring slid out of the wall with a grating noise that sounded like thunder.

Tad leapt forward and shook the ring under Cissie's nose. Immediately, she began to soothe Khush.

"Steady there. Well done. Steady."

But there had been too much noise to ignore. The dogs were flinging themselves at the gate, barking frantically. The sleepy stable boys shouted uselessly for a moment. Then one of them kicked the dogs into silence and shuffled across the yard. The gate creaked open.

"What's going on? Where's Mr Jackson's boy?"

Tad held his breath. Cissie nudged him, but she couldn't tell him what to say.

"Hallo!" he called weakly.

"What's up with that elephant of yours?"

"He's – er – he's nervous. Misses Mr Keenan."

The stable boy snorted. "Then give him some of

that medicine Mr Jackson was trying to sell us. Cures everything, by all accounts."

"I'll – I'll try—"

Tad was hoping the stable boy would give up and go away. But Cissie, beside him, suddenly clenched her fists and began to shake with silent fury, and that set Khush off again, trumpeting and rattling his chain.

"Are you sure that elephant's all right?" the boy asked suspiciously. "Maybe I ought to come and take a look."

"You needn't bother," Tad said. "He's just—"

But he could hear the boy shuffling over the cobbles muttering as he came closer.

"Where are you, you ugly creature? You can't be very – aargh!"

The last word vanished in a scream of terror, followed by the noise of running feet. Thudding into the gate, the boy scrambled through and crashed it shut behind him. Tad could hear the others laughing as he gasped out his story.

"Creature caught me a wallop round the head with that trunk! It's a savage brute! *You* can go and see it, if you like, but I'm keeping away. I'm paid to look after horses, not wild animals."

There was a roar of laughter, and more barking. Under cover of the noise, Cissie grabbed Tad's sleeve and whispered in his ear. *She* wasn't laughing.

"Did you hear? The man's even tried to steal my elephant tincture? Well, we're not leaving it for him. Have you got it in your hut?"

"We can't take that!" Tad said. The bottles were packed in two big, wooden boxes, roped together for slinging over Khush's back.

"They're *mine*. Go and get them!"

As Tad ducked into the hut, the face he pulled was hidden by the fog. He slipped the ropes over his shoulder and staggered out again with the boxes. For a moment, he couldn't work out where Cissie was. Then she called, from Khush's back.

"I'm up here! Pass them up."

Tad heaved the first box high enough for Cissie to reach. She dropped it over Khush's neck and settled the second one in its place.

"Now follow!" she hissed. "Carry the chain."

With the rusty iron ring in his hand, Tad padded behind Khush, across the damp cobbles and through the rickety gate at the back of the yard. He had no idea where they were going, or what Cissie's plans were. He followed blindly.

"We'll keep by the river," she whispered from above. "That way we're sure to walk out of town, and not back into it."

That sounded like a stopgap plan, born of the fog. Tad felt uneasy, but arguing would have made too much noise. Even the sound of Khush's shuffling feet seemed deafening and he was certain that people would hear their voices if they kept talking. He kept his worries to himself and followed.

They edged along the alley and out towards the river. A fresh, muddy scent seeped towards them, mixing with the smell of coal, just as it did along the Tamaquon river, on the edge of Markle. Tad caught the familiar whisper of fast, high water rushing through tall plants.

A foot at a time, without seeing where they were going, they made their way out of Pittsburgh. Tad tried to imagine what would happen when daylight came and the fog cleared.

Mr Jackson would be after them, the second he missed Khush. And they wouldn't be hard to follow. They must have left footprints, and enough of a scent for a clever dog to trace.

He called up, towards the dim shape on Khush's back. "Where are we going?"

Even through the fog, he could see how impatiently Cissie turned. "Where? Up river, of course. The river must come from the mountains. If we follow it, we'll be able to get back over them."

"But it'll soon be light."

"Then we'll find a barn to hide in."

A barn? Tad knew plenty of barns, but he'd never

known one where an elephant could hide unnoticed. And were they going to *walk* back over the mountains?

"Well?" Cissie snapped. "Have you got a better plan?"

"I—" Tad stuttered and fell silent. How could he make a plan? He couldn't even walk across a room without doing something wrong. It was far better to keep quiet and obey orders.

But Cissie had snapped louder than she meant to. Away to their left, a light flickered and a few seconds later a voice called out.

"Hey? *Wer ist das?*"

Cissie threw her shawl over the lantern and she and Tad froze. Khush turned towards the voice and flapped his ears, but he didn't make a sound.

The man called again. "I woke three times tonight already. It is enough. Your noise was joking?"

He sounded irritable and determined. Slowly, the light of the lantern grew closer.

"What for a joke is that, that wakes an old man?"

Tad's mind raced, but there was nothing he could do. Their best chance was to keep very still and hope the old man missed them in the fog. Any movement was sure to give them away.

The lantern stopped, moved sideways and came towards them from another angle. And, suddenly, he was there. A tall, gaunt old man, peering out of the fog not ten feet away from them. His hair hung long and grey on either side of his face and his dirty, worn shirt flapped out over his trousers.

Lantern held high, he stared at Khush with wide, disbelieving eyes.

"*Lieber Gott!*" he breathed. "*Lieber Gott in Himmel!*"

Cissie reacted while Tad was still catching his breath.

"Please!" she said. "Oh, *please!*"

She swung her leg over Khush's neck and slithered eight feet to the ground, falling into the pool of lantern light in front of Tad. The old man held out a hand to pull her up, and she grabbed it with both hers.

"Please hide us! I don't know who you are, but you have a kind face! We're being followed by enemies who want to steal my elephant and there's no one else to help us!"

By the end of the speech she was on her knees, looking pleadingly up at him. The fog swirled round her and the yellow light fell bright on her tumbled hair and her small, desperate face.

The old man looked bewildered. "I'm thirty years here – and I never saw a child with an elephant."

"He *is* my elephant!" Cissie said earnestly. "He's

all I have, in the whole, wide world."

"It's the truth," said Tad.

"There is a boy also?" The old man peered forward into the fog. "Come here, boy!"

Nervously, Tad walked into the light.

"Closer!"

The old man shook his hand free of Cissie's and beckoned impatiently. When Tad was within reach, he grabbed his chin and jerked it round, so that Tad was forced to stare straight into his eyes.

"What is it that she tells me? There are enemies?"

"Not enemies exactly—" Tad began to gabble. "A man says he bought the elephant from Cissie's father – just before the crash – but the money was an insult – and the writing on the paper was the wrong colour – and—"

His stuttered words dissolved, ridiculously, into silence and he wondered why he had spoken at all.

The old man's watery grey eyes scanned his face. "I see that it will take much telling. Perhaps you shall take the elephant into my barn. Then we may talk."

"Oh, thank you! Thank you!" Cissie jumped up and clasped her hands under her chin. "I *knew* you had a kind face. Come on, Tad. We're safe!"

Safe? Tad thought of dogs, and hesitated.

"It is not well?" the old man said. He was watching Tad very closely. "You do not trust me?"

210

"Of course I do. But—"

"But nothing!" Cissie said impatiently, scowling at him. "Don't waste time, Tad. They'll be after us as soon as it's light."

The old man held up his hand. "First we will hear the boy. What troubles you?"

"W-well," Tad stammered. It felt wrong to argue with Cissie, but he had to say it. "If they follow *us*, they may bring dogs. And the scent will stop here. And—"

The old man gave a long, slow nod. "That is careful. I like a careful boy. Take the elephant on, upwards of the river, and then return. We shall wait here."

Cissie pushed her lantern into Tad's hands. "Go on, then. I'll stay and explain everything."

Tad hadn't expected to be sent on his own, but he didn't dare to argue any more. He lifted the lantern high, trying to see Khush's head.

"Move up. Let's get going."

His voice sounded feeble and uncertain, drifting uselessly into the fog. Khush turned towards Cissie and flapped his ears.

"Move up!" Tad said, more firmly.

One huge foot rose into the air. Slowly, tugging at the water plants as he went, Khush ambled on up the river.

Before they had gone twenty yards, the old man's lantern was invisible. For a few steps more, Tad could hear the ride and fall of Cissie's voice as she began her explanation and then that, too, disappeared. There was nothing but the rush of the river and the shadowy bulk of Khush as he moved steadily along the bank, his feet squelching in the wet mud.

Once or twice, lights glimmered, far to the right or left. Twice, river creatures scuttled out of the undergrowth and dived into the water. For half a mile or more, Tad peered into the fog and strained his ears to catch every sound.

It was an empty world, where the two of them walked alone, wrapped up together. When Tad gave the order to stop, he said it without thinking, as he might have spoken to a person.

"Steady. Stop now, Khush."

The words sounded piping and thin, but Khush stopped straight away and Tad smiled.

"Now we're going to fool Mr Jackson."

For a second he wondered what he was doing, talking to a dumb creature. But out there, in the fog, it seemed the natural thing to do. Khush bent his head and his little eyes gleamed in the lantern light.

"We're going to walk back with our feet in the water, so that we don't leave footprints. So get over now."

Khush's trunk tickled him behind the ear.

"Stop playing around. Get over!"

The trunk tickled him behind the other ear, and he almost wished that he had the bullhook. He didn't know what would happen if he lost control.

"Khush!"

Dipping his trunk into the river, Khush pulled it out and squirted the ground, just in front of Tad's feet.

"You—!" Tad jumped backwards.

Immediately, Khush dipped his trunk in once more, and sent a new jet of water hissing on to the ground. Just missing Tad again.

It was impossible not to jump back. And straight away more water hit the ground, on the very spot he had just left.

He was being teased.

There was no mistaking it. As he backed away, step by step, Khush squirted again, with a perfect aim. Never hitting Tad's feet, but always close enough to make him jump away.

When Tad had been teased in school, it was always meant unkindly. And Aunt Adah had never had time for anything except work. This game was gentle and amiable, and for a moment he was completely bewildered by it.

Then, suddenly, he imagined how the two of them

must look. A boy and an elephant, standing alone in the fog and playing with water. Forgetting all about where he was, and who might be listening, he started to laugh.

As though that was what he had been waiting for, Khush veered right, and splashed down into the river. It was much deeper than Tad had expected. A wave lapped over the bank and for a second Khush disappeared completely under the dark water, medicine boxes and all. Then he surfaced, like a small island, with water streaming from his body.

"This way. Come here, Khush."

Walking backwards down the bank, Tad called softly and Khush began to plod steadily after him, parting the water like a barge, while Tad held the lantern high to keep him in sight.

It seemed a long time before they saw the answering lantern, and heard Cissie call.

"Is that you, Tad? Come to the ramp."

There was a curious, cobbled ramp leading up out of the river. It looked like some kind of slipway. Tad couldn't quite make out what it was for, but he was glad there was somewhere that Khush could climb out without marking the bank.

"I've explained *everything*," Cissie said eagerly. "And Mr Nagel says Khush can hide in his barn until tomorrow night."

Tad looked over her shoulder, at the old man.
"Thank you very much." He had not realized, until
then, how cold and tired he was. "Get over! Up on the
bank, Khush!"

"Come here, Khush!" Cissie said. "Come to the
barn."

Khush heaved himself out of the water, huge and
dripping, and marched up the ramp, his chain
scraping on the cobbles. Tad pulled a stray branch
from the flood debris caught in the reeds and brushed
away any stray elephant prints as he followed.

"A good, careful boy," said a voice behind him. Mr
Nagel was watching, with the lantern held high and

a strange, sad smile on his face. "Miss Keenan is lucky for a friend."

It seemed odd to be called Cissie's friend. Awkwardly, Tad swirled his branch again, wiping out the last print. Then he turned and stepped into the barn.

It was a large, solid building, set well back from the river. But its doors hung askew on their hinges and it smelt of neglect. Old, rotting sacks were tossed into one corner, and mouldering harnesses drooped on hooks, above a stack of withered roots.

The most curious thing of all hung from the roof. It was a long wooden platform, with a high raised edge, and it was suspended by ropes tied to its four corners. Tad took a few steps nearer, frowning up at it, and he heard Mr Nagel chuckle drily.

"You do not know what is that? Ha?"

"Is it some kind of grain store?"

"I use him for a grain store now. See the rings, to stop rats climbing down the ropes? But in the beginning – no, it was not for that." Mr Nagel's face twisted.

"Looks like a giant box," Cissie said flippantly. "Have you got a lid for it?"

Mr Nagel looked at her for a moment. Then at Tad. Then he marched down the barn and began to unwind one of the ropes. "I will show you."

There was a peculiar grimness in his voice and Cissie moved closer to Tad. "Do you think he's – all right?"

Tad looked down the barn. One corner of the platform was hanging free now, and Mr Nagel was panting slightly as he struggled with the second rope.

"Don't think he'll do us any harm," he whispered back. "And we've got nowhere else to go."

Grunting as he took the strain, the old man let out the second rope. One end of the wooden platform swung loose and rattled down to the ground, hitting it with a thump. Khush raised his trunk and snorted loudly, stamping his feet on the floor of the barn.

"Well, boy?" said Mr Nagel, gasping from the effort. He stepped back and gave Tad a challenging look. "What for a grain store is *that*?"

Tad walked slowly down the barn until he was standing at the lowered end of the platform. As Cissie had said, it was like a box. A shallow wooden box, around twenty feet long by ten feet wide. In the centre was a roughly built clapboard hut, with a single window and a pitched roof.

"Looks like—" He hesitated. What he was thinking seemed too strange to be true.

"I can see in your head," Mr Nagel said sadly. "You think like all my neighbours, that I am an old crazy. The man with a boat in his barn, instead of good cows."

Tad shuffled uneasily. The old man's pale eyes were fixed on his face, waiting for something.

"Why shouldn't you have a boat?" Cissie said briskly. "You're here by the river. You might as well row out on it from time to time. Don't you think so, Tad?"

Tad looked at the wooden box. He'd seen flatboats like that on the Tamaquon, and he knew what they were for. Not the kind of rowing picnic that Cissie had in mind. They could only travel down river, with the current. On one-way journeys.

Mr Nagel was still watching him. Tad stuttered out the question in his mind.

"Are – are you fixing to go west? Is that why you built it?"

"West?" The old man said the word bitterly, as if it were a lemon in his mouth. "What is *west* for a man with no sons? When I had two boys like you, *then* I was fixing to go west. With Franz and Heinrich – and Greta." He gasped a little, catching his breath.

"I'm sorry," Tad said, "Did they—?"

Cissie scowled, warning him to stop. Mr Nagel's face had gone stark white, with the beard stubble standing out dark and ragged. But he went on talking as soon as he could speak.

"They told me – after the cholera – that I should take a new wife. Make new sons. As if – as if a man could forget, and wipe away what has been."

Cissie sidled close to Tad again, and he saw her eyes widen nervously, but Mr Nagel didn't notice. Whatever he saw, it was not the two of them. It was not even Khush, tweaking shrivelled turnips from a sack. He tugged at his ragged grey hair and looked at the flatboat.

"A man with two boys has a reason. He can build such a boat. He can take all he owns – cows and chickens and pigs – and set off light in the heart. But a widow man? A childless man?"

He looked at Tad hungrily, searching for something that wasn't there.

"I'm sorry—" Tad said.

Mr Nagel shook his head. "I told you already – I am an old crazy. But I like to tell my tale. And to show my poor little craft, who will never go down the river now."

He picked up one of the slack ropes and began to tug at it, heaving the flatboat back up towards the roof. Tad went to help him, gripping the rope and pulling in time.

As the end started to lift from the floor, Khush ambled forward to examine it, idly tossing out a few wisps of hay that he found inside.

And in that instant, as Khush stood there and Mr Nagel and Tad hauled on the rope, Cissie yelled.

"No! Don't pull it up!"

"What?" Tad turned to stare at her. "What's the matter, Cissie?"

She didn't answer. Instead, she came forward and grabbed the old man's sleeve. "Did you say that people take animals in boats like that? Cows? And horses?"

Mr Nagel blinked at her, bewildered by her fierceness. "Of course. I have seen it many times."

"Then it's not a poor little craft!" Cissie said triumphantly. She laid a hand on the flatboat's wooden side. "It *can* go west. Give it to us, and we'll take it!"

"West?" Tad's head spun. "But we're going east, Miss Cissie. Over the mountains."

"Not any more!" Cissie was bubbling with excitement. She ran her hands lovingly over the flatboat. "Don't you see? We can put Khush in here and disappear down the river."

"You mean—" The whole thing sounded impossible. Tad couldn't believe she meant it.

But she did. She gripped his shoulder and spun him round, so that he could see Khush and the boat together. And her voice was fierce and determined.

"We're going to Nebraska!"

The Making of Parrot

Ted Hughes

In the beginning, there were even more song contests than there are now. All the creatures were just finding their voices for the first time. They were quite amazed at the sound that came out of their mouths.

"Listen, listen to me! Listen, listen, listen to me!" they were crying. Each one wanted all the others to listen. Wolves yelled, Toads quacked, Nightingales gurgled, Alligators honked, and the Leopard made a noise like somebody sawing a table in half.

"Listen to me," roared the Leopard. "Oh, oh, listen to my song! Oh, oh it makes me giddy with joy! Just listen!" And he went on, sawing away. It sounded wonderful to him.

But nobody was listening. Every other creature was too busy singing – head back, mouth wide, tonsils dancing. The din was terrific.

At least, it was so till the Parrot began. But at

Parrot's first note, all the creatures fell silent. The Demons under the earth fell silent. The Angels in the air fell silent. And the Parrot sang on alone. Even the trees listened, breathless, to the glorious voice of the Parrot.

What a voice! Where had he come from? Who was this astounding person?

Man had just been persuading Woman to marry him. He was rubbing her whole body with coconut oil, so she glistened like a great eel. "Marry me," he said, "and I'll do this to you every day."

"Well," she said, "maybe."

She loved being rubbed with oil, but what did Man mean by marriage? That was a new word. "Marry?" What did it mean? She wasn't so sure she liked the sound of it. But she didn't want him to stop rubbing her with oil. So she said, "Well, maybe."

And that was the moment the Parrot began to sing.

Man stood up. Like somebody in a trance, he walked straight out through the door. He simply left Woman lying there, as if he had forgotten she existed.

"Hey!" cried Woman. "Come back. You haven't finished."

But Man was already outside, gazing amazed at the Parrot.

And the surrounding trees of the forest were loaded with birds of every kind, all gazing amazed at the Parrot. And in the lower branches of the trees, and between the trunks of the trees, all the kinds of animals were jammed together, in a great circle, gazing amazed at the Parrot.

Parrot surely was something to gaze at. He was actually a Dinosaur – but a truly beautiful specimen. He didn't look like a modern parrot. He was much bigger. He was quite a lot bigger than a Peacock. Nearly as big as Woman. And he was thickly covered with every-coloured feathers. These feathers didn't lie down smooth, like the feathers on the neck of a Hen. They ruffled out, like the feathers on the neck of a Fighting Cock. He looked like a gigantic Native American head-dress. His face was a huge flower of rainbow feathers. His legs and feet were thick with glossy feathers, that changed colour as he stamped about. All his body was fluorescent, and as he sang, taking deep breaths, and flinging out the great flame-feathers of his wings, he seemed to be lit from inside by pulsing strobe lights – red, then orange, then yellow, then green, then blue, then indigo, then purple – then a blinding white flash and back to red. Really magnificent! And all the time, his incredible song poured out.

What a song! The crowding creatures couldn't

believe it. It seemed to pick them up bodily. Their eyes boggled, their jaws dropped, and they felt like puppets being jerked by strings.

Man stared in delight. This was something new. What singing! What a marvel!

"Can you believe it? Just listen to it!" he shouted, turning to Woman, who was now leaning in the doorway, looking out sulkily. "Can you believe it?" Man almost screeched with excitement.

Woman frowned. She just went on leaning there, feeling dull. What was the matter with her? All the creatures of the earth were there, swooning at the singing of the Parrot. And there was Man, who was so clever at everything, standing overpowered by the voice of that bird. "What's so wonderful about it?" she kept thinking. "Why don't I like it? What's wrong with me? Maybe my ears are funny."

She did try quite hard to like the Parrot's song. She didn't want to be left out. She closed her eyes, and listened so fiercely her head began to ache. But it was no good. She simply couldn't like it.

But now Man was dancing around the Parrot, flinging up his arms and legs. "I can't believe it!" he screeched. "I can't believe it! This is ecstasy! Where have you been? Oh! Oh!"

That first evening, Man took Parrot into his house.

And until late in the night, the creatures all stayed where they were, crowded around Man's house, hearing Parrot's great song coming from inside. The house seemed to tremble and jerk with the power of it. And every now and again they would hear Man cry:

"Fantastic! Another! Another!"

Man was so delighted by is new friend that he invited Parrot to live with him for ever. "I'll supply all you need," he promised. "Whatever food you like. Shelter from the bad weather. And you can sleep in that bed."

"Which bed?" cried Woman. She was already fed up with this gigantic bird. Her head was splitting with his pounding songs. Man hadn't even looked at her for the last eight hours. And now –

"That bed, there," said Man.

"My bed?" she gasped.

"Why not?" asked Man. He had already drunk a lot of beer.

Woman choked. She was so furious she couldn't speak.

"And give our new friend another glass of beer," said Man.

Parrot stared at her. He could see very clearly that this Woman didn't like him one bit. But that didn't worry him. He ruffled his feathers. The crest on his head stood up straight, and his eyes, big and round and cold and deadly, like a Dinosaur's, stared at her.

"Don't think you can hypnotize me, you horrible Turkey," shouted Woman.

"Do as you're told," snapped the Parrot.

Man laughed and drained his glass. "More beer for his Lordship," he said. "And for me too."

Woman went to fill the beer-jug, but she was thinking what Parrot would look like with all his feathers plucked off. Behind her, once again, Parrot burst into song and the jug in her hand began to vibrate.

Next morning, all the contestants for the great song contest were ready very early, outside Man's house, and the crowd was even bigger than usual. The Fox and the Turtle were bustling about, taking bets. Some of the creatures were terrible gamblers.

Today, most people thought Lion would win. He had never entered before. He had been out there on the resounding plains, perfecting his mighty song, for years, and rumours had been coming in. "It's simply stunning," said the Zebra. "Knocks your head off," said the Gnu. Everybody could see, by the way he lay there, eyes nearly closed, one forepaw laid over the other, that he was confident of winning.

Beside him the Wart-hog sat looking very nervous,

twitching his ears and tail, occasionally shaking his head. Nobody had the slightest idea what to expect from him.

But next in line was the Giraffe. The general opinion was that Giraffe had no voice at all – she was simply dumb. Even so, the Burrow Owls put their bets on her. "She's not dumb," they said. "You people are the dumb ones, thinking she's dumb."

There were three others: a Cormorant, a Woodpecker and a Loon. Loon was thought to be pretty good.

At last, Man came out, scratching his head and yawning. Parrot emerged, and stood beside him. He looked as fresh as a giant firework in full blaze.

Usually, Man judged the singing at these contests. But now he spoke to the crowd. "You all heard Parrot singing last night," he said. "Never have I heard singing like it. We must all admit, he's in a class of his own. And so, today, I've asked him to be our Judge."

A Monkey clapped.

"Let's begin," said Parrot. "Cormorant first."

The Cormorant had been persuaded to enter by the Seagulls. He opened his beak, flapped his scraggy wings, and began.

"Aaaaaaaaaark!" he croaked, and stopped.

"Is that all?" asked Parrot, blinking his pebble eyes.

"No, that's only the beginning," said the Cormorant.

"OK," said Parrot. "Sing it to the end."

Cormorant stretched up his neck, shifted his feet, and croaked, "Aaaaaaaaaaark!" and stopped. "That's the end," he said.

Parrot stared at him.

"Next," he said. "Woodpecker."

Woodpecker set back his head and laughed. After three or four laughs he stopped, and peered at Parrot. "That's mine," he said.

Parrot blinked. "Loon," he said.

The Loon writhed. His long neck performed like a snake with the itch, then shot up straight, as his beak opened.

A howling mad laugh twisted out. A Wren fainted and Man felt a shiver go up his back. Woman poked her head out through the doorway, round-eyed.

Parrot nodded and smiled. "Giraffe," he said.

Giraffe swayed. What looked like a bubble travelled slowly up her neck. Giraffe opened her mouth, and after about six seconds burped.

A baby Chimpanzee turned a somersault and screeched, till its mother hit it.

"Is that your song?" asked Man. Giraffe nodded

gracefully, and lowered her thick, long eyelashes.

"Wart-hog," said Parrot.

The Wart-hog's performance was quite good. He whirled on the spot, fell on his back, threshed his legs, churned with his tusks, writhed and contorted in a cloud of dust, and all the time let out noises like a cement-mixer. At last he stood up panting. He was sure he'd won.

"Lion," said Parrot sharply.

Lion stretched, yawned, took a deep breath, then suddenly gripped the earth with his claws and roared. The blast knocked off several rows of birds, and Man grabbed the rail of his veranda. Parrot's feathers flattened for a moment, and all the baby animals began to cry till their mothers hushed them. Then everybody waited.

Parrot seemed to be thinking. Then he said, "The result of this contest is – Winner: ME!"

The Lion frowned. All the animals began to chatter. "How is that?" roared a voice. It was Lioness. "How can that be? How can you be the winner?"

"Because—" said Parrot. And suddenly he burst into song. He leaped out into the middle of the beasts. His feathers flamed and shook, his colours throbbed. His voice was not only utterly astounding, it was amazingly loud. Man shouted with delight:

"He's right. He's the winner!"

And Man began to clap. All the animals began to clap. And when Man began to dance, they all began to dance. Clapping they danced, and dancing they clapped, while the Parrot whirled and sang.

But Lion, Giraffe, Wart-hog and Loon stood apart in a group. "He's not a bird," said the Loon. "He's a lunatic!"

"I might have won!" snorted Wart-hog. "I was in there with a fighting chance!"

And Lion said, "Something will have to be done about this fellow."

But Giraffe stuck her head in through a side-window in Man's house, and saw Woman lying on the floor, weeping.

"Your husband has gone crackers," said the Giraffe. "It's that Parrot."

Woman looked up. "I'm leaving," she sobbed. "I've had enough. That Parrot is a monster. Have you seen its eyes? And is that supposed to be singing? It's made me deaf."

She began to push things into a suitcase. "Man was going to marry me," she cried. "Since that Parrot came he never even looks at me. The Parrot orders me about and I sleep on the floor. I'm off."

"Wait," said the Giraffe. "We have a plan."

It was true. The Giraffe may have been a dumb singer, but she was a clever planner.

"Wait till we come back," said the Giraffe. "Give us two days."

Woman sat on the bed weeping. She nodded wearily. "OK, OK. But two days is the limit."

The Giraffe, the Loon, the Lion and the Wart-hog went to God. They told him that Man was getting married to Woman and that he wanted God to be there. But he daren't ask. He was too modest. In fact, Man was a little bit afraid of God. So the animals had come to ask what Man didn't dare to ask.

"I'd like very much to come to that wedding," said God. "Woman is my favourite invention."

"But what he really wants," said Giraffe, "is for you to sing a song."

"What," asked God, "at the wedding?"

And Loon said, "Woman thinks that if you sing at her wedding, they will be happy ever after. She believes that. She's praying you'll come."

God laughed. "Simple!" he said. "No problem. When?"

"Tomorrow," growled the Lion.

The animals came to Woman, and explained their plan. "The wedding must be tomorrow," they told her. "And you must get that Parrot to sing." So the same night, when Parrot was fast asleep in Woman's bed, a great heap of glowing feathers, Woman got up from the dirt floor where she slept with the cat, and whispered to Man:

"You begged me to marry you, do you remember?"

He woke up and lay staring into the dark.

"What's that?" he said. He thought he was dreaming Woman's voice. So she said it again: "You begged me to marry you, do you remember? Did you mean it?"

"Yes!" he said. "Oh yes. If you will, I'll rub you every day with warm oil. Oh yes! Will you? Will you?"

"Tomorrow," she whispered.

He would have jumped out of bed for joy, but remembered the Parrot and lay silent. Then he said: "I'm sorry about the Parrot. But you know how I need music. I get carried away."

"If he'll sing at our wedding," she said, "I will try to like him."

By dawn, the news of the wedding had spread. The animals assembled from every corner of the forest and plains.

"What's this about a wedding?" cried Parrot, rushing back into the house. Man was already draped with honeysuckle, and he was rubbing Woman's body with warm oil. "It's our wedding day," said Woman. "Will you sing for us? Can you sing a Marriage Song?"

"Haha!" laughed Parrot. His eyes seemed to whirl, but they were actually darting to and fro. His feathers were a-tremble. "Sing a Marriage song?" he cried. "Only give me the chance!"

"Oh, I knew you would, Parroty," she cried, and flinging her arms round him she covered his feathers with oil.

As he stood at the river's edge, trying to wash the oil off, Giraffe came strolling up.

"Hello, Parrot," she said. "I expect you're looking forward to hearing the new singer."

Parrot blinked. "New singer?" he asked. "What new singer?"

"At the wedding," said Giraffe. "He's supposed to be simply the best ever. They say he's already here. Some animals persuaded him to come. I think Man was hoping you'd sing. It's going to be a mix-up. I expect it will end up with both of you singing."

Giraffe sauntered off, and Parrot glared after her. He was beginning to feel angrier and angrier. First, he was furious about the oil on his feathers. And twice as furious about this new singer butting in on his show. A new singer? The best ever?

Parrot knew what he'd do. He'd challenge this new singer to a Marriage Song contest, on the spot. And he'd flatten him. He'd just crush him with his Parrot Song-power. The poor fellow wouldn't even be able to croak.

So Parrot shook himself like a great, gaudy dog, and came up from the river raging with eagerness to challenge the new singer.

God arrived looking like a beggar. He told nobody he was God and nobody recognized him. He merely said he'd heard there was going to be a wedding, so he'd brought a present. It was a hive full of bees. Man had never seen such a thing.

Already the creatures were crushing tightly

around Man's house. And Parrot stood there on the veranda, staring hard at the Beggar. Could this be the new singer? He didn't look like much competition, if he was.

Man was impatient to start. But this was the first wedding ever, and nobody knew how to do it. Then the Beggar had a bright idea. He smeared Man's and Woman's faces with honey, from the hive. Then Man licked Woman's face and Woman licked Man's face, and when all the sticky sweetness was gone – that was it, they were Man and Wife. So simple!

"And now sing a song," roared the Lion.

The Beggar nodded and smiled. But before he could open his mouth, a bellowing shout came from the veranda: "Wait!"

All creatures looked at the Parrot. And as they looked at him, Parrot began to sing.

But from the first moment something was wrong. Something was stuck in Parrot's throat. He stretched his beak wide open, his feathers rippled and flared, his colours throbbed – but he choked. Finally he coughed and spat out – a Fly. A big Bluefly.

It buzzed on to the veranda rail, and sat there, cleaning the back of its neck. The Beggar nodded and smiled.

Parrot began again, but he'd hardly got into full voice before the same thing happened again –

236

another Fly, which joined the first.

Parrot braced himself in rage, and began again. His voice choked, grated, strangled, as he forced out his song – and Fly after Fly shot out, till the veranda rail was crawling with them, and Parrot's eyes were blood-red.

He gagged finally, and bent over, coughing drily – while Fly after Fly came whizzing out of his mouth.

"Perhaps while we're waiting," said the Beggar, "I could sing a little song."

And the Beggar began to sing. As he sang, the animals seemed to grow in size. Woman began to pant and cry. And Man too, he suddenly collapsed to his knees, and crouched there, his elbows on the ground, clutching the top of his head. And out of the ground all round flowers began to push up and open. Huge blossoms and tiny florets. And out of every twig in the forest clusters of blossoms burst and hung down. And out of the core of every flower unfolded a different Butterfly. And Butterfly after Butterfly came out of the flowers, just as Fly after Fly had come out of Parrot's mouth, till the air was full of Butterflies, that settled everywhere on the birds and animals and covered Man and Woman like a rich, quivering cloak.

Then the Beggar began to sing more strongly. And now Parrot seemed to clear his throat and let out a screech. He was trying to sing. Everybody could see he was trying to sing, but all that came out were not Flies now but more and more horrible screeches. And as he screeched he writhed. It was truly awful to watch him. His feathers now seemed to be real flames, devouring themselves. And the Beggar stepped towards him with his eyes shining and sang a great torrent of song straight at Parrot. The poor bird whirled and blazed and screeched, while his feathers scattered like burning embers from a kicked bonfire, and his body shrank. He was like a whirling Parrot being tossed, or maybe a Parrot being bounced on the end of an elastic.

Suddenly Woman ran forward. She ran fearlessly into the blast of the Beggar's song, and caught up the Parrot, and ran into the house with it, and silence fell.

When Man uncovered his eyes and looked up, he saw the incredible garden of blossoms and Butterflies. The Beggar had disappeared. Man went into the house looking for his new wife, and found her nursing the Parrot.

He could only just recognize the bird. It was no bigger than a small Monkey. Its feet were scorched, scaly twigs. Its face was a bent lump, like glass that had melted and hardened again. Its eyes were little marbles in ashen sockets. Only a few colours. Only a few feathers. And its voice – its voice was just the burned-out wreck of its song.

"Poor Parrot," said Woman. "Poor little Parrot!"

But gazing at the Parrot all Man could think about was the tremendous song of the Beggar.

How Brer Fox and Brer Dog Became Enemies

Julius Lester

When the animals started living here on Earth, something seemed to happen to them. Where before they had gotten along with each other, now they started having little arguments and disagreements. It was only a matter of time before they weren't much different from people.

Brer Fox and Brer Rabbit were sitting alongside the road one day talking about much of nothing when they heard a strange sound – *blim, blim, blim.*

"What's that?" Brer Fox wanted to know. He didn't know whether to get scared or not.

"That?" answered Brer Rabbit. "Sound like Sister Goose."

"What she be doing?"

"Battling clothes," said Brer Rabbit.

I know y'all don't know what I'm talking about.

You take your clothes to the Laundromat, or have a washing machine and dryer sitting right in the house. Way back yonder folks took their clothes down to the creek or stream or what'nsoever, got them real wet, laid'em across a big rock or something, took a stick and *beat* the dirt out of them. You don't know nothing about no clean clothes until you put on some what been cleaned with a battlin' stick.

Well, when Brer Fox heard that Sister Goose was down at the stream, his eyes got big and Brer Rabbit knew his mind had just gotten fixed on supper. Brer Fox said he reckoned he better be getting home. Brer Rabbit said he supposed he should so the same, and they went their separate ways.

Brer Rabbit doubled back, however, and went down to the stream where Sister Goose was.

"How you today, Sister Goose?"

"Just fine, Brer Rabbit. Excuse me for not shaking hands with you, but I got all these suds on my hands."

Brer Rabbit said he understood.

I suppose I got to stop the story, 'cause I can hear you thinking that a goose don't have hands. And next thing I know you be trying to get me to believe that snakes don't have feet and cats don't have wings, and I know better! So, if you don't mind, you can keep your thoughts to yourself and I'll get back to the story.

After Brer Rabbit and Sister Goose had finished exchanging the pleasantries of the day, Brer Rabbit said, "I got to talk with you about Brer Fox. He's coming for you, Sister Goose, and it'll probably be before daybreak."

Sister Goose got all nervous and scared. "What am I gon' do, Brer Rabbit? My husband is dead and ain't no man around the house. What am I gon' do?"

Brer Rabbit thought for a minute. "Take all your clothes and roll 'em up in a nice clean white sheet and put that on your bed tonight. Then you go and spend the night up in the rafters."

So, that's what Sister Goose did. But she also sent for her friend, Brer Dog, and asked him if he'd keep watch that night. He said he'd be glad to.

Just before daybreak Brer Fox crept up to the house, looked around, eased the front door open and slipped inside. He saw something big and white on the bed. He grabbed it and ran out the door. Soon as he jumped off the porch, Brer Dog came out from under the house growling and scratching up dirt. Brer Fox dropped that bundle of clothes like it was a burning log and took off! It's a good thing, too, 'cause it had taken Brer Dog four months to find somebody who could wash and iron his pyjamas as good as

Sister Goose, and he wasn't about to let nothing happen to her.

Next day when the news got around that Brer Fox had tried to steal Sister Goose's laundry, he couldn't go nowhere for a week. Brer Fox blamed Brer Dog for spreading the news through the community, and ever since that day, the Dog and the Fox haven't gotten along with each other.

Brer Fox couldn't prove it, but he knew Brer Rabbit had warned Sister Goose he was coming, and he made up his mind to get even. Brer Rabbit got word about what Brer Fox was thinking on, so he stayed away from his regular habitats for a while.

On this particular day he was somewhere up around Lost Forty and saw a great big Horse laying dead out in a pasture. Or he thought it was dead until he saw the Horse's tail switch.

Brer Rabbit went on his way, but who should he see coming toward him but Brer Fox!

"Brer Fox! Brer Fox! Come here! Quick! I got some good news! Come here!"

Brer Fox didn't care what kind of good news Brer Rabbit had. The good news was that he had found that rabbit! Just as Brer Fox got in grabbing distance, Brer Rabbit said:

"Come on, Brer Fox! I done found how we can

have enough fresh meat to last us until the middle of next Septerrary."

Brer Fox, being a prudent man, thought he should check this out. "What are you talking about, Brer Rabbit?"

"I just found a Horse laying on the ground where we can catch him and tie him up."

Sounded good to Brer Fox. "Let's go!"

Brer Rabbit led him over to the pasture, and sho' nuf', there was the Horse laying on the ground like he was waiting for them. Brer Rabbit and Brer Fox got to talking about how to tie him up. They argued back and forth for a while until finally Brer Rabbit said:

"Listen. I tell you the way we do it. I'll tie you to his tail and when he tries to get up, you can hold him down. If I was a big strong man like you, I'd do it, and you know, if I was to hold him, he would be held. But I ain't got your strength. Of course, if you scared to do it, then I reckon we got to come up with another plan."

There was something about the plan that Brer Fox didn't like, but he couldn't think of what it was. Not wanting Brer Rabbit to think he wasn't strong and brave, he said OK.

Brer Rabbit tied him to the Horse's tail. "Brer Fox! That Horse don't know it, but he caught!" Brer Fox grinned weakly.

Brer Rabbit got him a great, long switch and hit the Horse on the rump – POW! The Horse jumped up and landed on his feet and there was Brer Fox, dangling upside down in the air, too far off the ground for peace of mind.

"Hold'im down, Brer Fox! Hold'im down!"

The Horse felt something on his tail. He started jumping and rearing and bucking and Brer Fox knew now what was wrong with Brer Rabbit's idea.

"Hold'im down, Brer Fox! Hold'im down!"

The Horse jumped and twirled and snorted and bucked, but Brer Fox hung on.

"Hold'im down, Bred Fox! Hold'im down!"

One time Brer Fox managed to shout back, "If I got *him* down, who got hold of *me*?"

But Brer Rabbit just yelled, "Hold'im down, Brer Fox! You got him now! Hold'im down!"

The Horse started kicking with his hind legs and Brer Fox slid down the tail. The Horse kicked him in the stomach once, twice, three times, and Brer Fox went sailing through the air. It was a week and four days before Brer Fox finally come to earth, which gave him a whole lot of time to realize that Brer Rabbit had bested him again.

It took Brer Fox a while to recuperate, but that gave him a lot of time to scheme and plan on how

he was going to get Brer Rabbit.

The very first day Brer Fox was up and about, he sauntered down the road. Coming toward him looking as plump and fat as a Christmas turkey was Brer Rabbit.

"Just a minute there!" Brer Fox said as Brer Rabbit started to walk past without speaking.

"I'm busy," said Brer Rabbit. "I'm full of fleas today and got to go to town and get some ointment."

"This won't take more than a minute," Brer Fox answered, falling into step beside him.

"All right. What's on your mind?"

Brer Fox gave a sheepish grin. "Well, Brer Rabbit. I saw Brer Bear yesterday and he said I ought to make friends with you. I felt so bad when he finished with me that I promised I'd make up with you the first chance I got."

Brer Rabbit scratched his head real slow like. "Awright, Brer Fox. I believe Brer Bear got a point. To show you I mean business, why don't you drop over to the house tomorrow and take supper with me and the family?"

Next day Brer Rabbit helped his wife fix up a big meal of cabbages, roasting ears, and sparrow grass. Long about supper time the children came in the house all excited, hollering, "Here come Brer Fox!"

Brer Rabbit told them to sit down to the table, mind their manners, and be quiet. He wanted everything to be just right. So everybody sat down and waited for Brer Fox to knock on the door. They waited a long time, but no knock came.

"Are you sure that was Brer Fox you saw coming up the road?" he asked his children.

"We sure. He was drooling at the mouth."

No mistake. That was Brer Fox.

Brer Rabbit got out of his chair very quietly and cracked the door open. He peeped one of his eyeballs out. He rolled his eyeballs from one side of the yard to the other until they stopped on a bush that looked like it was growing a fox's tail. Fox's tail! Brer Rabbit slammed the door real quick.

247

Next day Brer Fox sent word by Brer Mink that he had been low-down sick the day before and was sorry he couldn't come. To make up for it, he'd sho' be pleased if Brer Rabbit would take supper with him that very same evening.

When the shadows were at their shortest, Brer Rabbit went over to Brer Fox's. He'd scarcely set one foot on the porch when he heard groaning from inside. He opened the door and saw Brer Fox sitting in his rocking chair, a blanket over his shoulder, looking like Death, eating soda crackers in the graveyard. Brer Rabbit looked around and didn't see any supper on the stove. He did notice the butcher knife and roasting pan on the counter, however.

"Looks like you planning on us having chicken for supper, Brer Fox," says Brer Rabbit like nothing was wrong.

"Sho' nuf'," says Brer Fox.

"You know what goes good with chicken, Brer Fox?"

"What's that?"

"Calamus root! Seems like I can't eat chicken no other way nowadays." And before Brer Fox could blink, Brer Rabbit was out the door and into the bushes where he hid to see if Brer Fox was sho' nuf' sick.

A minute later Brer Fox come out on the porch

looking as healthy as a rat in a tuxedo. Brer Rabbit stuck his head out of the bushes and said, "I leave you some calamus root right here, Brer Fox. You ought to try it with your chicken tonight!"

Brer Fox leaped off the porch and took off after Brer Rabbit, but that rabbit was halfway to Philly-Me-York before Brer Fox's claws touched the ground. All Brer Fox had for supper that night was an air sandwich.

The World in a Wall

Gerald Durrell

The crumbling wall that surrounded the sunken garden alongside our house in Corfu was a rich hunting ground for me. It was an ancient brick wall that had been plastered over, but now this outer skin was green with moss, bulging and sagging with the damp of many winters.

The inhabitants of the wall were a mixed lot, and they were divided into day and night workers, the hunters and the hunted. At night the hunters were the toads that lived among the brambles, and the geckos, pale, translucent with bulging eyes, that lived in the cracks higher up the wall. Their prey was the population of stupid, absent-minded crane-flies that zoomed and barged their way among the leaves; moths of all sizes and shapes, moths striped, tessellated, checked, spotted and blotched, that fluttered in soft clouds along the withered plaster; the beetles, rotund and neatly clad as businessmen, hurrying with portly efficiency about their night's work. When the last glow-worm had dragged his frosty emerald lantern to bed over the hills of moss, and the sun rose, the wall was taken over by the next set of inhabitants. Here it was more difficult to differentiate between the prey and predators, for everything seemed to feed indiscriminately off everything else. Thus the hunting wasps searched out caterpillars and spiders; the spiders hunted for flies; the dragon-flies, big, brittle and hunting-pink, fed off the spiders and the flies; and the swift, lithe and multicoloured wall lizards fed off everything.

But the shyest and most self-effacing of the wall community were the most dangerous; you hardly ever saw one unless you looked for it, and yet there must have been several hundred living in the cracks of the wall. Slide a knife-blade gently away from the brick, and there, crouching beneath it, would be a little black scorpion an inch long, looking as though he were made out of polished chocolate. They were weird-looking things, with their flattened, oval bodies, their neat, crooked legs, the enormous crab-like claws, bulbous and neatly jointed as armour, and the tail like a string of brown beads ending in a sting like a rose-thorn. The scorpion would lie there quite quietly as you examined him, only raising his tail in an almost apologetic gesture of warning if you breathed too hard on him. If you kept him in the sun too long he would simply turn his back on you and walk away, and then slide slowly but firmly under another section of plaster.

I grew very fond of these scorpions. I found them to be pleasant, unassuming creatures with, on the whole, the most charming habits. Provided you did nothing silly or clumsy (like putting your hand on one) the scorpions treated you with respect, their one desire being to get away and hide as quickly as possible. They must have found me rather a trial, for I was always ripping sections of the plaster away so that I could watch them, or capturing them and making them walk about in jam-jars so that I could see the way their feet moved. By means of my sudden and unexpected assaults on the wall I discovered quite a bit about the scorpions. I found that they would eat bluebottles (though how they caught them was a mystery I never solved), grasshoppers, moths, and lacewing flies. Several times I found them eating each other, a habit I found most distressing in a creature otherwise so impeccable.

By crouching under the wall at night with a torch, I managed to catch some brief glimpses of the scorpions' wonderful courtship dances. I saw them standing, claws clasped, their bodies raised to the skies, their tails lovingly entwined; I saw them waltzing slowly in circles among the moss cushions, claw in claw. But my view of these performances was all too short, for almost as soon as I switched on the torch the partners would stop, pause for a moment, and then, seeing that I was not going to extinguish the light, they would turn round and walk firmly away, claw in claw, side by side. They were definitely beasts that believed in keeping themselves *to* themselves. If I could have kept a colony in captivity I would probably have been able to see the whole of the courtship, but the family had forbidden scorpions in the house, despite my arguments in favour of them.

Then one day I found a fat female scorpion in the wall, wearing what at first glance appeared to be a pale fawn fur coat. Closer inspection proved that this strange garment was made up of a mass of tiny babies clinging to the mother's back. I was enraptured by this family, and I made up my mind to smuggle them into the house and up to my bedroom so that I might keep them and watch them grow up. With infinite care I manoeuvred the mother and family into a matchbox, and then hurried to the villa. It was rather unfortunate that just as I entered the door lunch should be served; however, I placed the matchbox carefully on the mantelpiece in the drawing-room, so that the scorpions should get plenty of air, and made my way to the dining-room and joined the family for the meal. Dawdling over my food, feeding Roger, our dog, surreptitiously under the table and listening to the family arguing, I completely forgot about my exciting new captures.

At last, Larry, my older brother, having finished, fetched the cigarettes from the drawing-room, and lying back in his chair he put one to his mouth and picked up the matchbox he had brought. Oblivious of my impending doom I watched him interestedly as, still talking glibly, he opened the matchbox.

Now I maintain to this day that the female scorpion meant no harm. She was agitated and a trifle annoyed at being shut up in a matchbox for so long, and so she seized the first opportunity to escape. She hoisted herself out of the box with great rapidity, her babies clinging on desperately, and scuttled on to the back of Larry's hand. There, not quite certain what to do next, she paused, her sting curved up at the ready. Larry, feeling the movement of her claws, glanced down to see what it was, and from that moment things got increasingly confused.

He uttered a roar of fright that made Lugaretzia, the maid, drop a plate and brought Roger out from beneath the table, barking wildly. With a flick of his hand he sent the unfortunate scorpion flying down the table, and she landed midway between my sister, Margo, and my other brother, Leslie, scattering babies like confetti as she thumped on the cloth. Thoroughly enraged at this treatment, the creature sped towards Leslie, her sting quivering with emotion. Leslie leapt to his feet, overturning his chair, and flicked out desperately with his napkin, sending the scorpion rolling across the cloth towards Margo, who promptly let out a scream that any railway engine would have been proud to produce. Mother, completely bewildered by this sudden and rapid change from peace to chaos, put on her glasses and peered down the table to see what was causing the pandemonium, and at that moment

Margo, in a vain attempt to stop the scorpion's advance, hurled a glass of water at it. The shower missed the animal completely, but successfully drenched Mother, who not being able to stand cold water, promptly lost her breath and sat gasping at the end of the table, unable even to protest. The scorpion had now gone to ground under Leslie's plate, while her babies swarmed wildly all over the table. Roger, mystified by the panic, but determined to do his share, ran round and round the room, barking hysterically.

"It's that bloody boy again . . ." bellowed Larry.

"Look out! Look out! They're coming!" screamed Margo.

"All we need is a book," roared Leslie; "don't panic, hit 'em with a book."

"What on earth's the *matter* with you all?" Mother kept imploring, mopping her glasses.

"It's that bloody boy . . . he'll kill the lot of us . . . Look at the table . . . knee-deep in scorpions . . ."

"Quick . . . quick . . . do something . . . Look out, look out!"

"Stop screeching and get a book, for God's sake . . . You're worse than the dog . . . Shut *up*, Roger . . ."

"By the Grace of God I wasn't bitten . . ."

"Look out . . . there's another one . . . Quick . . . quick . . ."

"Oh, shut up and get me a book or something . . ."

"But *how* did the scorpions get on the table, dear?"

"That bloody boy . . . Every matchbox in the house is a deathtrap . . ."

"Look out, it's coming towards me . . . Quick, quick, do something . . ."

"Hit it with your knife . . . *your knife* . . . Go on, hit it . . ."

Since no one had bothered to explain things to him, Roger was under the mistaken impression that the family were being attacked, and that it was his duty to defend them. As Lugaretzia was the only stranger in the room, he came to the logical conclusion that she must be the responsible party, so he bit her in the ankle. This did not help matters very much.

By the time a certain amount of order had been restored, all the baby scorpions had hidden themselves under various plates and bits of cutlery. Eventually, after impassioned pleas on my part, backed up by Mother, Leslie's suggestion that the whole lot be slaughtered was squashed. While the family, still simmering with rage and fright, retired to the drawing-room, I spent half an hour rounding up the babies, picking them up in a teaspoon, and returning them to their mother's back. Then I carried them outside on a saucer and, with the

utmost reluctance, released them on the garden wall.
Roger and I went and spent the afternoon on the
hillside, for I felt it would be prudent to allow the
family to have a siesta before seeing them again.

ACKNOWLEDGEMENTS

The publishers wish to thank the following for permission to reproduce copyright material

Gerald Durrell: "The World in a Wall" from ch. 9 of *My Family and Other Animals* by Gerald Durrell; first published 1956 and reproduced by permissioin of Curtis Brown Ltd., London on behalf of the Estate of the author. Copyright © Gerald Durrell.

Robert Westall: "David and the Kittens" from *Cats' Whispers and Tales* by Robert Westall; first published 1996 and reproduced by permission of Laura Cecil Literay Agency on behalf of the Estate of the author. Copyright © The Estate of Robert Westall 1996.

Noel Douglas Evans: "The Wire and the Woodpecker" from *Animal Stories* by Noel Douglas Evans; first published by Struik Publishers (Pty) Ltd 1995, pp. 7–18, and reproduced by permission of the author.

Ted Hughes: "The Making of Parrot" from *Tales of the Early World* by Ted Hughes; first published by Faber and Faber Ltd 1988, pp. 37–50, and reproduced with their permission.

Michael Morpurgo: "The White Horse of Zennor" from *The White Horse of Zennor* by Michael Morpurgo; first published by Penguin 1982, pp. 29–47, and reproduced by permission of David Higham Associates on behalf of the author.

Leon Garfield: "A Grave Misunderstanding" from *Guardian Angels: Fifteen New Stories by Winners of the Guardian Children's Fiction Award*; first published by Viking Kestrel 1987, pp. 9–14, and reproduced by permission of John Johnson (Author's Agent) Ltd on behalf of the author.

Christobel Mattingley: "Katzenfell" from *Eerie Tales*; first published by Hodder & Staughton Australia 1978, pp. 7–22, and reproduced by permission of the author.

Gary Paulsen: "Ike" from *My Life in Dog Years* by Gary Paulsen; first published by Macmillan Publishers 1998, pp. 19–37, and reproduced by permission of Flannery Literary on behalf of the author.

Philip Sherlock: "Tiger Story, Anansi Story" from *Anansi, the Spider Man* by Philip Sherlock; first published 1954 and reproduced by permission of Macmillan Publishers.

Books in this series available from Macmillan

The prices shown below are correct at the time of going to press.
However, Macmillan Publishers reserves the right to show new retail
prices on covers which may differ from those previously advertised.

Adventure Stories for Five Year Olds	0 330 39137 2	£4.99
Animal Stories for Five Year Olds	0 330 39125 9	£4.99
Bedtime Stories for Five Year Olds	0 330 48366 8	£4.99
Funny Stories for Five Year Olds	0 330 39124 0	£4.99
Magical Stories for Five Year Olds	0 330 39122 4	£4.99
Adventure Stories for Six Year Olds	0 330 39138 0	£4.99
Animal Stories for Six Year Olds	0 330 36859 1	£4.99
Bedtime Stories for Six Year Olds	0 330 48368 4	£4.99
Funny Stories for Six Year Olds	0 330 36857 5	£4.99
Magical Stories for Six Year Olds	0 330 36858 3	£4.99
Adventure Stories for Seven Year Olds	0 330 39139 9	£4.99
Animal Stories for Seven Year Olds	0 330 35494 9	£4.99
Funny Stories for Seven Year Olds	0 330 34945 7	£4.99
Scary Stories for Seven Year Olds	0 330 34943 0	£4.99
School Stories for Seven Year Olds	0 330 48378 1	£4.99
Adventure Stories for Eight Year Olds	0 330 39140 2	£4.99
Animal Stories for Eight Year Olds	0 330 35495 7	£4.99
Funny Stories for Eight Year Olds	0 330 34946 5	£4.99
Scary Stories for Eight Year Olds	0 330 34944 9	£4.99
School Stories for Eight Year Olds	0 330 48379 X	£4.99
Adventure Stories for Nine Year Olds	0 330 39141 0	£4.99
Animal Stories for Nine Year Olds	0 330 37493 1	£4.99
Funny Stories for Nine Year Olds	0 330 37491 5	£4.99
Revolting Stories for Nine Year Olds	0 330 48370 6	£4.99
Scary Stories for Nine Year Olds	0 330 37492 3	£4.99
Adventure Stories for Ten Year Olds	0 330 39142 9	£4.99
Animal Stories for Ten Year Olds	0 330 39128 3	£4.99
Funny Stories for Ten Year Olds	0 330 39127 5	£4.99
Revolting Stories for Ten Year Olds	0 330 48372 2	£4.99
Scary Stories for Ten Year Olds	0 330 39126 7	£4.99

All Pan Macmillan titles can be ordered from our website,
www.panmacmillan.com, or from your local bookshop
and are also available by post from:
Bookpost
PO Box 29, Douglas, Isle of Man IM99 1BQ

Credit cards accepted. For details:
Telephone: +44(0)1624 677237
Fax: +44(0)1624 670923
Email: bookshop@enterprise.net
www.bookpost.co.uk

Free postage and packing in the UK.